*Dedicated to my beautiful wife
and the six Impids with which
we have been blessed*

*I am overwhelmed with the kindness and generosity of all
who helped bring* Calapanta *to completion – a special
note of thanks to Anne Carroll and Barbara Mirus for
taking time out of their busy schedules to read and edit
the first draft; to Ben Baker for his suggestions in
improving the storyline; to Jack Murphy for providing the
artwork; to Chris Graham for his expertise in finalizing
the cover design; to my father, James Heisler, for his
loving patience during the countless hours he spent
pouring over the structural elements of the story; and,
finally, to my wife, Mary, for her loving support
throughout.*

CONTENTS

Part I

OF DREAMS AND DECISIONS

Part II

LUKE'S JOURNEY

Part III

HUN KANNY

Part IV

AT THE WATER'S EDGE

CALAPANTA

PART I

OF DREAMS AND DECISIONS

In vain you get up earlier,
and put off going to bed,
sweating to make a living,
Since it is he who provides for his
beloved as they sleep.
(Psalm 127:2)

Chapter One

WALKING TO SCHOOL

JIM'S FIRST day in tenth grade had finally arrived. His summer had been uneventful. Day had followed day in an unmarked voyage through time. And now he was walking the same path he had walked last June, with but a long slumber in between. But he told himself that *this* year would be different, that he was going to have a good start, a fresh start.

That's the reason he left home some thirty minutes earlier than usual. The extra half hour gave him plenty of time to think things over. Summer had begun with a boundless potential that boggled his mind. As it turned out, it was too mind-boggling, and he ended up following through on none of his plans. Instead he slept in until two or three in the afternoon each day and told himself that he would "start on it tomorrow". Then summer vacation ended.

It was one and a half miles to school, and his walk had only just begun.

"Today," Jim told himself as he dragged his feet up the hill, "I'll begin it today. I'm awake. I have second period study hall. No assignments yet – it should be a perfect time to start. Start school, start a story." One of the options Jim had considered over the summer was to start writing again: Not essays and term papers, but stories.

****

When he was in grade school, he loved to write about Hun Kanny. Hun Kanny was a giant Godzilla-like creature who would show up and save the day after some other monster had spent a good portion of that day ruining it. When in grade school, he had not cared that the concept itself was terribly unoriginal, nor that the story lines had all followed the same pattern, nor even that Hun Kanny himself had died at the end of three of his stories, yet somehow inexplicably continued to defend humanity against indescribable evils. He simply loved to write the stories and to illustrate them with crayon pictures.

Then came fifth grade. Hun Kanny had defeated everything from a three hundred foot snake named Sikili to a mad scientist named George, and the time had come to make a compilation. The young author organized the stories chronologically. In the absence of a time frame connecting one story to another, only he knew what "chronological" would be. But he did it, and was quite happy with the progression of battles. Then, using all the muscles he had in his 11-year old wrists, he stapled them together. This was an amazing feat in itself. The school's art teacher had a three-inch long stapler he would lend to the students. It was advertised as a safe, "kid-friendly" device, but its lack of force rendered it almost useless. Most students would resort to the "double-dog ear" method of attaching their pages after several failed attempts with this stapler. But Jim did not give up; he was on a mission, and by the time he finished stapling a binder down the side of *The Complete Adventures of Hun Kanny*, the stapler was ready for burial. The book, however, was ready for the public.

He presented it to his class, and when Scott Howard asked to take it home, Jim graciously said yes. Scott, he thought, would no doubt be enthralled with the literature and recommend it to Aaron who would recommend it to Mike, and so on and so forth until it became the most popular book at St. Mary's School.

Two days went by after he loaned the book to Scott, then three, then four. Friday had come, and Scott had yet to say a word about Hun Kanny. Jim had been letting him bide his time. He felt that if he pushed the issue, Scott would not be able to appreciate the book fully. Besides, something as substantial as *The Complete Adventures of Hun Kanny* would take anyone a few days, if they were truly to enjoy it. Of course the first reading would go quite quickly, but then the reader was sure to browse through several more times, taking in the brilliant illustrations, and pondering the depth of the more complex aspects of the stories. Jim also took into account the fact that Scott was not a fast reader. But by Friday, he could no longer contain himself.

"So, what'd ya think?"

"What'd I think about what?" came Scott's reply.

Jim was shocked, stunned. Scott had to be joking he thought. "What'd ya think about Hun Kanny?" Scott looked at him puzzled. "Hun Kanny... the book I gave you on Monday? – So what'd ya think of it?"

Scott could not possibly have known the gravity of the situation or he would not have replied so casually, "Oh, I lost it on my way home. Remember I told Mrs. Lacasse I lost my math book? I wasn't lying this time. I really lost it, and your papers were in it." It was at this moment that Jim realized the genius of a Xerox machine. He had given Scott the world's only existing copy of *The Complete Adventures of Hun Kanny*. "I'm an idiot!" he told himself. How could he have given the book to Scott! At eleven he was too old to be so careless, he thought. "First he loses my masterpiece, and then he calls it just a bunch of papers!" Scott had added insult to insult.

Jim pleaded with Scott to look for his math book. He reminded Scott every day of the next week, and every day Scott claimed to have looked for it. After that week was over, Scott said he was done looking. The book was never found.

Jim was left with only one story. "Hun Kanny vs. the Mad Scientist" sat in a drawer at home, and the only reason he hadn't stapled this into the book was because he thought it was poorly written. The rewrite, which he *did* like, had been put into the lost book.

The idea of writing all of his wonderful stories over again was just too daunting for the fifth grader. And so Hun Kanny, for all intents and purposes, had disappeared from the face of the earth without ever making his mark.

Then in sixth grade it looked as though the nail in Hun Kanny's proverbial coffin had been irrevocably hammered. Hockey had entered Jim's life, and he quickly fell in love with the position of goalie. It was new and inviting, different than anything he had tried before. And as it turned out, he was quite good. Thus any lingering ideas of childhood fantasy stories gradually faded away. They had been replaced by a new passion.

But Hun Kanny was not *quite* dead just yet. No, for three years the fantasy hero lay dormant; then, during freshman year, Jim's knees began to act up. As hockey season progressed, they rapidly grew worse. And soon he found himself in a doctor's office being told that he did not have "goalies' knees". According to the doctor, this was a fairly common occurrence among young goalies, and if Jim stopped playing hockey, his knees were sure to recover splendidly. If he did not, however, it would take double knee surgery before Jim could get suited up and back on the ice.

High school hockey had been a drastic change for him anyway. He was no longer the MVP goalie of a championship junior high team; he was now the big stuffed teddy bear at the end of the bench. So he quit. It wasn't the most honorable thing to do, he guessed, but knee surgery to continue as a benchwarmer in no way appealed to him.

Hockey was over.

The time had now come for Hun Kanny to reappear. Several months earlier Jim's mother handed him "Hun Kanny vs. the Mad Scientist". While tidying up his room, she had come across it in one of his drawers. She thought he would like it. He didn't. In fact, it was worse than he remembered. But its discovery awakened long forgotten dreams of Hun Kanny.

As Jim's freshman year came to a close, he decided to resurrect his hero. During summertime "The Adventures of Hun Kanny" would return. They would not be the same, for there was no way he could remember exactly what Hun Kanny had done more than four years ago. It was a shame, he thought; but he could write new adventures, better, more exciting adventures than ever he could have conceived in fifth grade.

****

Those new and better, more exciting adventures never did arrive. And when August ended, Jim had not written one sentence. So his decision to start the story during study hall of that first day of his sophomore year was of personal significance. It meant to him that he was not giving up on Hun Kanny. For some reason, it gave him great pleasure to know that Hun Kanny had not been doomed to the great trash heap of discarded ideas which rotted in the back of his mind. Every once in a while he would rummage through this mental landfill of decomposing conceptions, but no idea, not one, was ever revived. He felt that Hun Kanny had been snatched, rescued in the nick of time, from the refuse in his cerebral garbage truck, before it unloaded its compiled junk from the summer to make room for the coming school year.

As Jim made his way to school on that first day of his sophomore year, he considered the various adventures Hun Kanny would have. With which would he start? Which monsters should survive from of old, and which new ones should make a grand debut? "And his flame needs to be cool," he thought. Since Hun Kanny was entirely imaginary, he could blow any color fire Jim desired. This was something different from fifth grade. "The story's already better," he mused. "In order to make it more realistic, I'll just ask someone in chemistry class which gases give off weird colored flames." In that case, he thought, a pouch will be necessary. It would have to be made of special protective tissue, and it would be attached to Hun Kanny's trachea. The pouch, filled with the special gas, would, of course, have an epiglottis-like barrier to prevent the gas from pouring into Hun Kanny's lungs. It would only open when he wanted to exhale fire and would quickly close again.

Jim was still going through the different colors in his mind – deciding between green and purple, as it so happened – when he saw someone, visibly drenched, walking his way.

It was *him*...

Chapter Two

STUDY HALLS AND DREAMS

DRAGONS WERE *everywhere.*

"No... that doesn't work!" Jim scratched his pen violently on the paper until the words were covered over in black ink. He looked up at the study hall monitor who was busy with some writing of her own. Consumed by her unfinished class preparations, she seemed oblivious to the students.

As Jim stared ahead, his eyes began to burn. He was battling fatigue, a peculiar fatigue that had been steadily growing since midway through first period, and now it was beginning to overwhelm him. But he refused to give in...

The young warrior looked into the sky and saw the red flame spewing forth from the largest creature he had ever laid eyes upon.

He sat back, content with the sentence he had just written. Yes, this sentence, at least, was a good one. It was a good opening to...

And his burning eyes forced their way shut. They had a will of their own by now, a will determined to sleep. But Jim continued the battle. Giving his head a violent shake, he pried his eyes open and again looked up at the study hall monitor. She was still focused on her work. It was the first day of school, and the study hall had begun with a brief introduction, which included the expectations the monitor had for the students. There was to be absolutely no talking or whispering she had said. This was to be a "silent" study hall. Then she informed them that she had "a lot to do," and trusted that they would keep themselves busy as well with work of their own.

Jim was experienced enough to realize that she was new to teaching, or new to study hall monitoring at any rate. First, he was fairly certain that maintaining a "silent" study hall was an active job – not one that can be accomplished staring down at the teacher's desk. Second, expecting students to "keep themselves busy" during study hall on the first day of school was grossly naive. Many of the students weren't going to "keep themselves busy" during a second period study hall on any day of the school year.

Thus far, however, he had been quite surprised by the results. The first half of the period had been exceptionally silent. But now twenty minutes had gone by, and the rumblings of discontent could be heard brewing in the back of the classroom. Soon the monitor would have to take a more aggressive approach to maintaining a good studying atmosphere. This, of course, would make it much more difficult for her to accomplish the work she had intended to do during the period. For the present, however, she continued looking down, writing at her desk.

Then the giggling commenced. It started soft and reserved from somewhere in the back corner. Quickly it grew much more unrestrained, and Jim's ability to concentrate on the story was severely hampered. He found himself staring blankly at the large, green chalkboard in front of him wondering how the monitor could get any of her own work done. When she eventually did look up Jim looked down, and the reprimands began. He could see the template for study hall sophomore year being created. The classroom was filled with gigglers; she was an inexperienced monitor. The same pattern was sure to be followed every day.

He sat quietly listening to the monitor scold her study hall and pondering how he could possibly have the flu on the first day of school. After many threats she managed to regain silence, if only for a few moments. And when the episode was over, Jim found himself thankful in one respect. The electricity of the entire event had woken him up. Once again, he picked up his pen intending to write but still found it difficult to focus. Something deeper was preventing him, something which he had been trying desperately to force out of his mind.

He wasn't ready to revisit the morning's conversation just yet, the conversation he had had with *him*. Yet, as absurd as it was, it wouldn't go away.

Putting his pen in his mouth, Jim chewed on its cap, wondering whether he should give it any credence.

"No," he concluded, "jumping in the river still makes no sense." But if that were so, why did it continue to plague him?

Sleep was beginning to return, and it became increasingly difficult for him to reason his way through the puzzle. "Why didn't I jump?"

The first thoughts of "duty" sprang up. No, he knew that if what he had been told were true, then it would be his "duty" to jump into the river. His brain, as foggy as it now was, could still see that much.

"Because it wasn't true; that's why I didn't jump... because it couldn't be."

Deeper, he felt there was another reason for his failure to jump, and it had nothing to do with "duty" at all. It had to do with a lack of trust... and with fear; at least that was the best way he could describe it – the simple fear of being taken for a fool.

But was it that simple? If he had jumped in, and it was all a big lie...

He looked down at the single sentence scrawled on his paper.

The young warrior looked into the sky and saw the red flame spewing forth from the largest creature he had ever laid eyes upon.

The decision to start writing again, this decision he had made with such conviction just a short while ago, had not panned out as expected. That morning, when he first woke up, he thought he would be able to sit down during study hall and, with all the latent creativity built up from three months of untapped imagination, write feverishly until the bell ended the period. Instead, as he listened to the study hall testing its waters, he sat staring at a mostly blank sheet of paper, searching for answers he doubted he would ever receive. And the bell rang ending second period.

Jim picked up the sheet.

"Tomorrow had better be quieter, or detentions will fly," warned the study hall monitor.

It didn't appear as though the students were deeply affected by this admonition. They happily chatted away as they walked out of the classroom. Jim wondered if any of them ever paid attention to what the others were saying. He crumpled the sheet and stood up to go to the next period, English 10. As he made his way toward the door, he found his energy had been completely sapped. There was no way he could make it through another period. His head ached, and it was an effort to walk. Fatigue had clearly overpowered him. "The flu," he thought, "on the first day of school."

If he went to the school nurse, the rest of the day would be spent trying to decide what to do with him. Neither of his parents was home at the moment, and the nurse would not allow him to walk there by himself, especially if he were sick. However, it *was* a large school. He decided that if he snuck out one of the doors, no one would notice.

As he walked by the trashcan exiting the room, he threw the wadded up sheet of paper away... "So much for starting my story," he grumbled.

He trudged along down the hall, entered the boys' restroom, and locked himself in one of the stalls. Then he waited. When the bell rang beginning third period, he began to rethink his decision to skip school, but then, persuading himself that nothing important happens on the first day anyway, he left the restroom, walked down the empty hall, went through the doorway, and made his way home.

Though he never liked to miss school, even *if* he were sick, something about that bizarre morning had made him too tired to survive the day. He was going to have a difficult enough time "surviving" the trip home.

By the time he arrived at his front door he was almost too exhausted to walk. It had been one and a half miles of drudgery that had felt like a marathon. With nobody there to question him, he unlocked the door, labored across the kitchen, and started up the stairs. He began with slow, slumberous steps but ended with a death-like crawl. Several times along the way, he stopped and nearly gave in to temptation. For sleep beckoned. The soft carpet had grown irresistibly alluring, and the distance to his bed seemed to grow rather than diminish with each passing stair. But he yearned for his bed, for his pillow, and continued on. The last stair finally conquered, he crawled to his bedroom. Then slipping victoriously under his covers, he closed his eyes and promptly fell asleep.

****

THE DREAM began with an excited buzz at school. Someone had started a rumor about the discovery of a certain cloak which enabled its wearer to fly. Evidently, in order for the cloak to work, the wearer had to jump off the top of Lookout Rock, located near Jim's house.

Jim lived on a dead-end street that was an offshoot of a longer dead-end street. This longer street made its way up a steep hill until it terminated at the forest. A tortuous path began here, which meandered upward through the forest to the summit of the hill – Lookout Rock. Its name was derived from the fact that there, hidden amongst the trees, one could see much of the town. For years the adolescents of the town had talked about hang gliding from this spot, but nobody had actually done it. It was a steep drop down for three or four hundred feet before the decline became less severe. It was not exactly a precipice, but the descent was over jagged rocks and splintered stones. If one were miraculously to survive the fall, he would have very little skin left attached to his body.

By the end of the school day, however, talk of Lookout Rock and the cloak had died down. Jim told himself that he hadn't believed any of it in the first place. He hated to look like a fool joining in the fray of fresh gossip. And, above all, he hated being gullible. So instead he decided to play pickup basketball; 3 on 3 with some of his friends. But he couldn't seem to make any shots or even focus on the game, and eventually he wandered away, not sure where exactly he was wandering, yet content to wander. And as he made his way up the dead end street and through the woods, he knew where he was going.

When he reached the top of the hill and stood at the edge, he noticed that Lookout Rock had somehow become a full-fledged cliff looking out at the sea, and, standing there, he listened to the sound of the waves crashing against the base. For some reason this did not strike him as odd. Nor did it surprise him when a stranger walked up next to him and smiled. He knew this must be the owner of the cloak, so he backed up and waited. And even in the dream, he was reminded of the morning's conversation, but could not put his finger on exactly why. The man stood still for about five minutes. Jim wanted to scream out, "Jump already!" but managed to refrain. Then the man took out a red cloak from a bag he was carrying and slipped it on. He turned to Jim, gave him a wink and leaped off the edge. Jim had expected a prologue of some sort, a big fuss to be made; not just a wink and off he goes.

But there he was, flying out over the water. Jim couldn't help but watch; he watched the entire show, dumbfounded, as the man sailed through the air. And then the man came back. Jim couldn't believe that anyone who had the opportunity to fly like that would come back in so short a time.

"Why'd you stop?" he asked.

"It looks like thunder," said the man.

Jim stared up at the sky. There wasn't a cloud; clear blue spread to the horizon. "What d'you mean?" he laughed, "There aren't even any clouds."

"You don't understand" was all the man said. Then he turned and walked away.

Immediately, Jim knew what he had to do. Hiding amongst the trees along the way, he followed the man. And when he saw where the cloak was kept, he ran back to the five boys with whom he had been playing basketball and told them his plan: After midnight, Aaron, the smallest and fastest in the group, was to slip into the man's house, grab the red cloak, and race to Lookout Rock where he would meet the rest of them. It wasn't terribly complicated.

They then split up and went home. When the time came each escaped unnoticed from his house. Jim was in a state of disbelief as they scurried up the hill to the cliff, gasping for breath. Aaron met them before they had made it to the top, and he had the red cloak in his hand! They had succeeded!

An argument ensued concerning who would be the first to go. Each one wanted to, but at the same time the risk of jumping off the cliff was a bit daunting. When Jim finally said, "Alright, I'll do it," this bolstered the others' courage; they were not so afraid that they would freely let him go first. After a few rounds of rock-paper-scissors, it was decided that Mike would go first. In fact, the complete order was decided in this fashion, and Jim was last.

"That's not fair!" he complained. "The whole thing was my idea!" This received a not-so-polite request for him to be quiet. The finality of rock-paper-scissors was not to be questioned. Thus, left with no other way to influence the order, he silently accepted his position.

Mike's hands were shaking as he put on the cloak. He walked slowly to the edge, and, with an awesome leap of faith, he leaped off the cliff. They could see him sail far into the distance, come back, fly close to the edge, turn and sail away again. Then, after several rounds, Mike landed.

Fear was gone. The moon shone brightly in the clear night sky, and none of them were in a hurry to end their flights. So, after only three had had their turns, dawn arrived, and it was time to go home. Before they left they decided to reassemble their clandestine little group that night at the same time. All agreed. The three who hadn't flown yet would go, and the others were excited at the prospect of a second round.

Jim was put in charge of hiding the cloak. He tucked it under his bed and lay down hoping to get a little sleep, but before he could close his eyes his mother was knocking on the door. He immediately checked under the bed to see how visible the cloak was and decided to stuff some dirty shirts around it. She knocked again informing him that it was time to get up. When he finally opened the door, she asked what took him so long. He collected his thoughts for a second and then told her he had a headache, hoping this lie would get her off his back; it did.

He could feel his heart pumping in his chest just thinking about flying that night. Obsessed with the cloak, he could think of nothing else all day. Several times his younger brother tried to talk to him, but he rudely told him to go away. His mother asked him to help around the house by doing the laundry or washing dishes or vacuuming. Each time he refused, repeating the lie about his headache. He spent the entire day in his room. When his father arrived home from work and announced that it was time to pray the rosary, he thought the night would never come. He tried to tell his father that he was too tired. None of his friends had to do a rosary, and he didn't want to do one, not now. He wanted to go to Lookout Rock to fly. But when he tried to speak, no words came out.

Chapter Three

AWAKING AND REMEMBERING

HIS MOTHER shook him. "Jim," she whispered, "it's time to wake up, honey." He turned to look at her, but his eyesight was blurred. As he tried to focus she spoke to him again, still whispering, "Pauly said you were sleeping when he got home. Are you feeling okay?"

"I don't know, Mom," he said groggily. "I think I am; it's just..." He yawned before continuing. "I was so tired I had to come home and get some sleep."

She pressed her lips to his forehead. "You don't feel hot," she said, no longer whispering, "but you look very pale. Are you sure you're okay?"

"Yeah, Mom – really. I'm feeling a lot better." Both his head and his eyesight were beginning to clear.

"Well, I know how you hate to miss school, but I'm sure you can catch up on anything you missed tomorrow. I just hope you're not sick."

"Mom, I'm fine. And it was only the first day. I don't think I missed much."

"Well, sometimes the teachers like to jump right in..." she began, then, seeing his eyes roll, she quickly changed the subject, "Do you think you can come down for the rosary? Papa's home and it's time to start. That is... if you're feeling up to it."

He scratched the side of his head for a few seconds, thinking it over. "Yeah, give me a minute," he decided. "I'll be right down."

"I'll tell Papa to wait for you." Then she kissed his forehead again, repeated "You look awfully, awfully pale," and left.

Although Jim could be easily annoyed by his mother at times, he truly loved her. And he could never lie to her, at least not as he had done in the dream. "I'm glad it was only a dream," he thought, "...but it would have been fun to fly."

When Jim went downstairs, his father took a look at him and said that it was probably a one-day thing, nothing to be too concerned about. Then the family prayed the rosary. When they had finished they sat down for supper.

The evening felt a little odd to Jim. On the first day of school, the two children would usually tell their parents about their new teachers, classes, and anything else about the new school year. Pauly was able to do this. But Jim contented himself with listening to the family discussion. He decided that it would be prudent not to mention what he had done, or *might* have done, that day. When asked what his morning was like, he told the truth: "I made it through second period and then got so tired I could barely walk any more. I don't know if I got some sort of weird sickness or what... I'm sure I'll feel better tomorrow – like Dad said." And with that the conversation ended. The inner debate to tell his family the full truth about that morning did not end, however. It seemed most unwise to talk any further about it, but at the same time, it seemed dishonest not to.

Jim not only loved his mother, he loved his father and brother as well. He especially loved suppertime. His mother was an excellent cook, and his father was an excellent storyteller. The two children would enjoy eating their food as they asked their father about his day at work. And as he told them story after story, they would laugh, sometimes teary-eyed, until their stomachs hurt, thinking their father had the best job in the world. It was not until years later that they discovered the truth – any job their father had would have seemed like the best job in the world. He happened to be a pathologist, but he could have been a traveling salesman. It was his unique way of seeing the world that made it so awfully funny.

Then after supper, it was time for catechism. The two boys would lie against the couch, as their father would sit on it asking questions. The information was transferred through repetition, but it was never dull. He brought the same sense of humor he had at the supper table to the living room couch. Tonight, however, was proving difficult for Jim. He didn't know how this morning's adventure meshed with everything he had learned in these catechism classes. He wasn't sure if it were even possible for the things he had been told to be true. The desire to ask his father grew stronger as time wore on, but he couldn't think of a safe way to phrase the question. And he began to question his own mental stability when he realized how insane it would all sound.

Distracted as he was, he repeatedly gave wrong answers, but his father didn't push him. Pauly picked up the slack. He would laugh and then answer the question correctly. Jim knew it made Pauly feel somewhat accomplished to be able to answer any question his older brother had missed. And Jim continued distractedly missing them right down to the last question he was asked: *Is it possible that there are intelligent beings created by God on other planets of the universe?* Jim said no. Again Pauly laughed at him and yelled out "Of course it is!"

"Yes; it is possible," his father read, "that there are intelligent beings created by God on other planets of the universe, because God's power is unlimited."

"Hold on," Jim was obviously paying attention now. "So, is it possible that there could be these doorways we read about in fantasy stories?" He asked the question before he realized what he had done.

"Possible," his father answered, "possible... but not probable." Jim shook his head, and with that catechism was over. His father looked at him and said, "I think it's time for you to go to bed, Jimbo. You still look rather pale."

Jim agreed. He was still feeling drowsy and had no desire to be exhausted again tomorrow. So he went to bed. However, when he placed his head on his pillow fully expecting to drift off to sleep, he found himself unable to do so. The morning's conversation was returning to him with exceptional clarity, and he pondered his father's words: "Possible... possible..."

What if Kor had been telling the truth all along?

****

JIM WAS *still going through the different colors in his mind – deciding between green and purple, as it so happened – when he saw someone, visibly drenched, walking his way.*

It was him.

Jim recognized him immediately. And before he knew it, he was following the boy toward the public library, which he was passing on his right. They didn't enter the library. Rather they went into the forest behind it. There was a thick line of trees running from the rear of the building. It was rough going negotiating all the branches, but once through, they would be secure from any disturbances. Here, the boy stopped, waiting for Jim.

****

TWO YEARS earlier, one of Jim's classmates had mysteriously disappeared. It had made all the papers in the county. He even remembered seeing a couple of specials on the news concerning the event. It seemed that the classmate's mother, uncle, and two of his cousins had vanished without a trace as well.

The boy had sat on the other side of the classroom from Jim, so the two did not talk during school. And outside the classroom, they never saw each other. But it still shook Jim up when one day, whish! The boy was gone. The news programs had made a big to-do of the whole ordeal, because a similar tragedy had occurred to the boy's father several years earlier. His father, whose name happened to be Jim as well, was eventually declared dead.

The boy's aunt was questioned extensively and claimed ignorance. Everybody believed her, for she was visibly distraught. Then, as a final punctuation to the entire event, she followed suit two months later. This led to a whirlwind of chaos for a couple of weeks. News cameras and reporters flooded the small Maine town. There were rumors of everything from twisted cult rituals to extraterrestrial abductions to the family themselves being Martians. Jim's father had been much more down to earth. According to him, the family probably snuck off to Aroostook County and started a new life farming potatoes. Reporters, he had said, love to dramatize everything.

Then one day, the media left for Boston, drawn by the '86 World Series. One tragedy had supplanted another, it would seem. And midway through his eighth grade year the town had subsided to being the same old town, though the mystery remained unsolved.

Jim remembered thinking the classmate was a bit eccentric, that he had an "overactive imagination" as the adults would call it. The other boys in the class used to make fun of him, not because he wrote fantasy stories, but because he actually pretended to live them. By seventh grade this was deemed immature behavior, and unacceptable to peers who focused on winning their next game, whatever the sport might be. Jim was a little jealous of the boy for his ability to shut out the insults and enjoy his own imaginary world. But, of course, he had become too involved with the game of hockey to have time for such things.

In fact, Jim had become so involved with hockey that he had forgotten about the boy entirely. That is, until this morning.

****

THE TWO teenagers huddled together as if they had just stolen a pack of cigarettes, about to sneak their first light. Jim began whispering. "Where've you been?" was all he could manage.

"We don't need to whisper," he was told.

"Oh... I thought... maybe someone'd hear us?" said Jim.

"No. Not here." The two stopped huddling and stood up straight. Then the boy sat comfortably with his back to a tree trunk, and Jim sat next to him. The boy's clothes dripped, dampening the dirt beneath them. "We're safe. Nobody's looking back here."

"Where've you been, Kor?" Jim repeated.

Kor paused for a second. "I've been away," he said, evading the question. "...But, I came back because I need to talk to you."

Jim was baffled. "Why me? I hardly even knew you."

"But I knew *you*, at least well enough," Kor assured him. "You're the one I need to talk to... Jim, listen," and just as Jim was starting to get his bearings back, to feel as if this weren't all a dream, Kor said, "Hun Kanny's real."

Jim knew he *should* have been surprised by this. As a matter of fact, he should have been incredulous. But he wasn't. Instead, he felt that he was indeed in a dream, a dream where the incredible is true.

"You've seen him?" he asked.

"No. No, I haven't."

Jim wouldn't have been surprised if Kor could have described Hun Kanny right down to his brand new pouch attached to his trachea. But Kor hadn't seen him at all, and this *was* a surprise. "Uh..." It was Jim's turn to pause, as his face betrayed his confusion. "Then how do you know he's real?"

"Let me take you back a little bit. Remember when I used to get made fun of for living in my own little world?" Jim nodded. "Well, I don't think you're ready to believe me, but I'm going to tell you anyway: my own little world is actually the big world – it's reality. Most people just don't know it."

"Kor – I was one of the people who used to make fun of you. Don't you remember? I mean, I'm sorry now, but I used to make fun of you a lot."

"Of course I remember," Kor cut in, "but that doesn't change anything... I know it's hard to accept, but think about this – first of all, I'm here. And second, Hun Kanny's been on your mind. There's a reason for that too."

This stumped Jim. Until now, he had been harboring the idea that Kor could quite possibly be insane. But that didn't explain how he knew what Jim had been thinking. Jim was quickly realizing that much of the conversation could not be explained. "You're not a potato farmer are you?" he asked.

"No... why?"

"I don't know, I thought maybe..."

"Jim," Kor interrupted, "it's the connection... your connection with Hun Kanny. That's why I'm here. Trust me. It's got nothing to do with potato farming."

"So, what do you want me to do?"

"Well... you need to meet him."

Jim said nothing, so Kor repeated himself. "You... you *have* to meet him."

"Meet him?" said Jim. "How am I supposed to do that?"

"By doing what I ask," said Kor. "In case you didn't know, you're not the only one who has a schwah."

"What?"

"I said, 'By doing what...'"

"No, after that – what did you say I had?"

"Hun Kanny. He's a schwah," repeated Kor. Jim chuckled, rolling his eyes, and Kor lost his patience. "Everyone's so blind! Look, there are a lot of schwahs – each one's different... I don't know, for some reason I thought maybe you'd know some of this."

"No. Actually I don't. The only schwa I know is the upside down 'e'," retorted Jim.

Kor didn't respond, so Jim continued. "It's the pronunciation symbol in the dictionary... the 'uh' sound. Come on," he teased, "– as smart as you were?"

"Jim... you asked how you could meet Hun Kanny, and I told you – by doing what I ask. Now, are you going to listen or not?"

"Yeah," answered Jim, "I'm listening."

"Like I said, each schwah is different, but none of them can talk. Instead, they find other ways to communicate.

Mine's learned to write. He can write even quicker than I can read. But you've got to remember, each one's different. They communicate differently. Do you understand?"

Jim didn't.

"Hun Kanny's the one who put himself in your mind all those years ago. It's not so much you thinking of him as him thinking of you. And those stories you wrote. You were getting to know him... he was getting to know you. He's real Jim – I can't lose you on that."

After finishing, Kor stared silently at Jim's unresponsive face. Neither of them spoke for a while. Jim could tell that whatever was happening, Kor was taking it very seriously. He had come back after two years of absence to talk about Hun Kanny.

The more Jim thought about it, the more mysterious his relationship with this "imaginary monster" became. He had always taken it for granted, but now it made little sense to him, and he broke the silence. "How did I develop a 'connection' with a creature I've never seen?" he asked.

"Yes, you have," said Kor, "Close your eyes and picture him." Jim closed his eyes. "Ever wonder why you can see him so easily?" asked Kor.

Although he was lost for an explanation, he had to admit he could see Hun Kanny quite clearly. In fact, he had known what Hun Kanny looked like for as long as he could remember.

"But I've never *actually* seen him," Jim stammered.

"That's not important; the point is he's real... and you need to meet him."

"Why?" Jim was slowly beginning to believe.

"I don't have time to explain it all here. We need to go to the river."

"Why the river?" questioned Jim. Then he looked at Kor's wet clothes. "Is that where you came from?"

"No, it's not... But we need to go there. Too much is depending on this... I know it sounds ridiculous, but it's true... I need you to stop living in this little box of a world... Deep down you know it's true. Hun Kanny and you *have* to meet." He was emphatic. "Too many people are depending on you. And most of them don't even know it."

"What's that supposed to mean?" asked Jim.

"I can't tell you any more," said Kor. "I really can't. All I know is that it's time to meet Hun Kanny..."

"Don't you think I want to meet him? Of course I do! But you come back after two years and tell me a bunch of weird stuff and expect me to buy it all? I'm supposed to be at school in a few minutes, not here or down by the river... It's not a very good start to the year." His desire to meet Hun Kanny was being overtaken by logic. "So if I'm gonna go to the river and get in all this trouble, could you at least give me some kind of reason? Maybe tell me where you've been for two years?"

"I understand this is all very bizarre, and that your head's spinning a bit, but there isn't much time," answered Kor. "If you come with me to the river, I'll explain what I can along the way?"

Jim agreed; he wasn't sure why, but he did. He followed Kor across the street, through the park and down the western bank. The stupor which had begun when he first met Kor began to grow, and he listened with the feeling that this was all terribly unreal, yet peculiarly inviting. As they hurried along Kor explained where he came from – it was a place inhabited by people called Impids... yes, they were humans just like Jim, and they lived in the Amazon, but, no, it wasn't the Amazon from South America.

Confused, Jim interrupted and asked for an explanation. "Exactly!" said Kor. "If I was making all this up, you think I would've named it 'the Amazon'?"

"No... But then, why do they both have the same name?" asked Jim.

"I'm not sure," Kor told him. "I think it's somehow connected to the Greek myth. A lot of the Impids think *it* inspired the *myth*. And they all agree that, in a roundabout way, the Amazon you know was named after theirs."

After this brief digression, Kor returned to the business at hand: Kor's schwah, whose name was Hives, watched over the Impids as their protector. However just as there were good schwahs, like Hives and Hun Kanny, there were also bad ones – corrupt ones that could cause the destruction of entire cities.

At this point Jim could no longer contain himself. "Come on... this sounds like one of my stories!"

Kor continued leading the way, "It's not. It's real. They're real. Hun Kanny's real. And he needs you, Jim. He needs you now."

"Okay. So what do I do?" asked Jim.

"Trust me... that's what you need to do right now. My guess is one of these bad schwahs is loose, and since no one's seen Hun Kanny, there's nothing to stop it. You see, you're it. You're the only one who can get a hold of him."

"Why can't *you* do something with *your* schwah?" asked Jim.

"I don't doubt Hives could help, if he could get in," said Kor. "But he can't."

"What do you mean Hives can't get in?"

"It's impossible. It's not his domain. It's Hun Kanny's."

Jim's curiosity led him to his next question. "Okay, then what do these 'bad schwahs' look like? What exactly am I supposed to be facing?"

Kor slowed down his pace, "You've seen dragons, right? Not the nice and cuddly ones, but the evil ones, the really evil ones? You know what I'm talking about?"

Jim tripped a little when he heard this. "They look like dragons?"

"No," replied Kor, "They are dragons."

BY THIS time, they were standing at the edge of the river.

"Now you need to trust me," said Kor.

"You're about to tell me to jump in."

"That's right. See that rock in the middle – the one that just breaks the surface at its peak?" Jim nodded. "Well if you swim to the bottom you'll find a huge hole dug out of the rock."

"So you want me to swim to the bottom of the river looking for a hole in the rock... dressed like this?"

"Yes. Swim through the hole to the other side," Kor continued, undaunted by the question.

"Why am I supposed do this?"

"Because, right now, your door is so *easy* to get to. It's your door, yours and Hun Kanny's. It's not mine. I can't go through. It's not always this easy. And if you don't go now, it'll be nearly impossible to get through later. You'd have to jump off Memorial Bridge to get enough force... And you're needed on the other side."

"What do you mean 'other side'?"

"When you come to the surface, you won't be in Maine anymore."

This shook Jim awake. "Wait...wait a minute. 'Doorway'? That's *really* original... this is like every fantasy book ever written. They all have doorways to 'fantastic new dimensions'."

"Of course," responded Kor, ignoring the exaggeration, "they're imitating reality. They always do... Ever ask yourself why so many fantasies have doorways?" Kor paused, but Jim, imagining the question to be rhetorical, waited for the answer. "It's because they exist... maybe not like in the books, but they exist."

"What about elves and wookies?" questioned Jim. "They're in fantasies."

"What I'm telling you is that a lot of things exist that people don't believe. And doorways are one of them."

Jim had to admit, he was becoming intrigued. "Okay, then how *do* they work?" he pressed.

"I don't know," answered Kor. "Nobody does, at least nobody I've talked to. But that doesn't mean they don't exist."

"Then how come more people don't know about them?" asked Jim.

"Because they're hidden. There's something," he paused searching for the right word, "... something mystical about them. I'm willing to bet more people have gone through than you think.

"I *have* learned this: there are two types. There's a general one... that's the type I used today. Anyone can go through these. That is, anyone except schwahs. But there aren't many of these left. The other one's more specific – like the one in this river. You can go through it, and so can Hun Kanny, but if *I* swam through that rock," he said pointing to the river, "I wouldn't go anywhere... It's yours, and you have to go through it..."

"But why do I have to go through it *now*?" interrupted Jim. "Why would it be impossible later on?"

"Nearly impossible," corrected Kor. "Your door expands and contracts. Later on it'll be hidden under the river bed up that way," Kor thumbed upstream. "That's why it'd take quite a jump to get down into it. Right now, though, it's expanded out to the rock, but it won't stay there for long. It's *your* door, Jim, and *you* need to wake up Hun Kanny. I can't."

"What do you mean, 'Wake up Hun Kanny'?"

"When a schwah's forgotten as long as you've forgotten Hun Kanny, he falls into a deep sleep. It's almost like he's dead. And you're the *only* one who can wake him up."

"Well, how am I supposed to do that?" asked Jim.

Kor thought for a second before responding, "All I can tell you, is when you get there... you'll know."

Jim looked out across the river for a couple of minutes and imagined jumping in to search for the hole under the rock.

He couldn't explain any of this: how Kor knew so much about his life, where Kor came from in the first place, or why he had followed him to the river instead of walking to school as he had planned to do when he woke up this morning. But now was the moment of truth, and he was finding it difficult to make himself jump in. He felt as though he was beginning to come to, to wake from the spell under which he had been cast. And Kor's explanations suddenly seemed terribly wanting, dubious even. When the plan was still in the theoretical stage it seemed exciting. But now that it was about to happen, it had lost much of its flavor. Kor knew that Jim had been thinking about Hun Kanny, and that was all. It wasn't much compared to what Kor was asking *him* to believe. And the longer he stood on the bank, the more it seemed completely absurd. He was late for school, and he was not going to make it worse by chasing after some childhood fantasy at Kor's bidding. No, he would not jump into the water.

Kor had been standing next to Jim, quietly waiting. Then, out of the corner of his eye, Jim saw Kor turn and slowly walk away.

"Where're you going?" he asked. When Kor looked back, Jim could see his disappointment.

"I couldn't believe this would happen," Kor said. "I simply could not believe it – you're not going to jump in."

"Well, I'd like a little more information than 'I don't know'. You've told me nothing about the other side except 'scary, scary dragons'." Jim was trying to sound practical.

"I can't give you more. You need to go. That's all I can tell you. You need to wake up Hun Kanny... We're in this together Jim. But I can't make you jump in. I can't force you to do your part. I can't force you to wake up Hun Kanny. It's all you." He was slow and direct with his next question. "Are you going to jump?"

Jim was annoyed at the directness, so his answer was curt: "Actually, no, I'm not." Immediately he felt like taking it back, but instead he continued, trying to justify his statement. "Look, this is stupid. The reality is I should be in school, but instead I spent my morning with you, and then you bring me here to jump into the river dressed in my school clothes, as if it's the most natural thing in the world. But it doesn't stop there. No. You want me to go searching around the bottom of the river for a hole that's supposed to lead me to some fantasy world. I'd drown before I ever found... hey, where're you going?"

Kor turned to face Jim one last time: "You need reasons? You need explanations?" he said. "Sorry Jim – can't do it. But I've got bad news for you. You can only live in your little box for so long. Time's running out. So you stand there, stand by the river's edge refusing to jump in – needing your explanations, needing to understand everything... You're forty feet from Hun Kanny you fool! You've dreamt about him your whole life... and it's forty feet! If I was forty feet from meeting Hives, I'd... but I guess you're different... everybody is." He paused for a moment. "I could argue all day... you wouldn't listen." With that he pivoted and walked away.

Jim wanted to follow him. He wanted to ask him more questions. He even *wanted* to jump in. But somehow, he couldn't. He imagined drowning... or worse, coming up on the other side, and looking around at the east side of the town, and he couldn't handle that. Everything Kor had said had seemed totally ridiculous, yet at the same time, it had made sense. Jim wanted to believe, but he was simply too afraid to put his trust in something unbelievable and then find out all of it was false. That would be more than he could bear. No, it wasn't that he wouldn't jump in; it was that he couldn't jump in. He wanted to scream back at Kor and tell him how much he wanted to believe him, how much he wanted to jump in, but he silently let Kor walk away. He knew that nothing he could say would change anything. He failed to trust. The least he could do was not try to rationalize that away.

He stood there for ten more minutes trying to convince himself that he was making the right decision. The whole idea began looking sillier and sillier. Drenching his clothes to risk his life in some fanciful underwater quest was not looking any more reasonable now than it did when he had first arrived at the river's bank. Kor had disappeared he knew not where, and he began to wonder if Kor had been real in the first place. This struck him as impossible, but then, so did everything that Kor had told him. He laughed at himself, "For a second there, I truly believed that Hun Kanny existed." The entire episode was quickly transforming into a dream. The more he thought about it the more preposterous it seemed, and he laughed again, for it had suddenly become entirely comical.

With this last chuckle it was his turn to leave. He began slowly walking to school...

****

AND THAT was it. That was the conversation from beginning to end, just as bizarre as ever. Jim shook his head; still no answers. Then he turned over and, for the second time that day, fell asleep.

Chapter Four

CRASH LANDING

THE DREAM resumed rather abruptly with Jim
sneaking out the window. He had tucked the cloak inside his
shirt to hide it. As he placed his foot on the ground he stepped
on a dried twig, which snapped, breaking the dark silence of
the night. He stood motionless, waiting for someone to wake
up, but nobody did. So he continued on toward his secret
rendezvous. This time, when he arrived at Lookout Rock, he
saw a wooden fence surrounding it. It crossed his mind that he
should have noticed this fence before. The entrance was about
ten feet wide, and was set roughly fifty yards in front of the
cliff. It had an old-fashioned wooden gate that swung inwards.
The gate was already opened. The fence itself spread out
widely until both sides terminated at the cliff's edge some
three hundred feet apart. He stopped briefly in front of the
opening, shrugged his shoulders and entered.

All of his friends had made it. They surrounded him
to make certain he had the cloak. The huddle was tight and
growing tighter when he exposed the red cloak to the night air.
It was a vision! A manifestation! And they backed away to
see the cloak in all its beauty as Jim shook it out, revealing its
fullness.

The impact of the cloak's exposition eventually waned, and it was time to fly. The night was beautiful; the full moon illuminated the forest around them, and its reflection softly swaying on the sea below could be traced to the horizon; the stars were myriads of delicate candles flickering in the heavens, smiling down on the cloak and shimmering on the waters.

It was even better flying weather than the night before!

Jim remembered that he was last, so he reluctantly gave the cloak to the fourth person on the waiting list. He put it on and dove straight down toward the rocks at the base of the cliff; then just as he was about to make contact, he leveled out, and they could hear the high pitched squeal of his laughter. He then began to soar toward the horizon, and eventually disappeared into the moonlight. Every so often they could just make out his body floating over the calm waters in the distance. Finally, he returned to the precipice handing the cloak to the next man.

After an eternity of waiting, the fifth person was back and was removing the cloak. Everything seemed in slow motion as pangs of impatience ran through Jim's bones making him nauseous. Finally, it was off! Jim grabbed for it anxiously, afraid it would disappear before his very eyes. But it didn't. No, it was in his hands! It was over his shoulders! At last, the magical cloth covered his entire body!

The time had now come for him to fly. His friends bade him hurry, for they all wanted a chance to go again, but Jim would take his time. Of that he was sure. He leaped, crossing the threshold from ground to air, and panicked. Flapping his arms like a large rooster, he attempted to gain some sense of equilibrium. Eventually, he realized that the best thing to do was to let go. He relaxed and began to float gracefully through the night air. He could feel the wind play with his hair as he enjoyed the scenery. Slowly he drifted far away. As he listened to the rolling waves of the water below him, he felt timeless. Then he began to feel pleasantly inebriated and could no longer think straight. He couldn't even remember how many people were waiting for him back at Lookout Rock, nor did he care. An ethereal, almost ineffable joy consumed his body. He turned over and floated face up, staring at the moon, pondering heaven. He decided that this was indeed paradise, and that as long as he was clothed with this burnoose he would be detached from anything earthly... Burnoose! He could not remember where he had heard the word before, but it was perfect! He would soar off to Arabia, cloaked with *his* burnoose, in search of a genie! In fact, he would do whatever he wanted. For, he suddenly felt that all his fantasies could now come true.

And with this last thought, everything went black.

The moon disappeared, and the stars were swept away as if by some great cosmic tail. Then came the thunder. Jim heard an explosion echo through the darkness, and he began to plummet. As he descended to the rocks below he remembered the words of the man who owned the cloak: "It looks like thunder." He hadn't understood until now, until he landed on the jagged stones at the base of the cliff.

The impact was painful, yet he somehow managed to land without breaking any bones. Then began his torturous ascent. The splinters from the rocks penetrated his skin as he clambered up the oddly sloped cliff. Groping his way through the darkness, he could feel that the incline was less severe than it had looked from the top. But still, the rocks continued gashing his knees and his elbows. All the while, an unsettling mixture of wailing and moaning and screeching persisted from above. The noise, slight at first, grew louder and louder as he made his way upwards. Distracted by this dreadful sound, he lost his balance and smashed his forehead. The blood ran down, burning his eyes, and he began praying for help. He prayed to his guardian angel; he prayed to the Blessed Mother; he prayed to God Almighty Himself. When he finished his prayers, it was time to quit. The excruciating pain of the shards in his hands had become unbearable, and the terrifying noise had become deafening. He decided to relax his body, allowing himself to roll down the cliff to be swallowed by the waters below. But before he released his grip he was suddenly filled with the urge to reach up for one more grasp. And as he did so his bloody hand clutched a clump of grass. It felt foreign at first, something he couldn't quite place. Then the realization hit him – he had made it to the top!

Slowly and awkwardly, he hoisted himself over the edge. Lying there for a minute, he caught his breath, then, carefully rising, he balanced on his feet to stand. Everything had gone silent, and he looked around to see what had been making that horrifying noise.

He closed his eyes tightly, as if to blink away the darkness. When he opened them he could see. But it was not with the clear light of the moon that he saw. It was more of a murky, hazy light, the source being something distant and weak.

Hoping to locate his friends, he immediately looked toward the opening in the fence. At first he could not make out what he was seeing. Either his vision was still too blurred or his brain refused to accept what stood there. However, as he regained clarity of vision and thought he could see that there, standing at the gate, was the cause of what had been a sickening din.

Four hooded creatures wore cloaks of their own: dark, ragged cloaks covering their bodies completely. The thought of flying away and escaping crossed Jim's mind. But when he looked down, he was surprised to find that the red cloak had disappeared. And staring back at the gate, he realized that no escape was possible. As his sight continued to sharpen, he saw red, menacing eyes staring out from within the dark shadows of their hoods. These things at the gate were piercing the night's darkness, searching, it seemed, for something yet undone. And each held an arrow to accomplish the task. Their four bows, however, had been left leaning against the wood of the fence.

Jim looked elsewhere, and, seeing the evil that these creatures had already accomplished, his legs froze fast with fear: to his left a head was affixed to the fence by an arrow – its attached body looked more like a stuffed scarecrow's than a human's; further along, a decapitated corpse drenched the grass with blood that oozed from its neck; next to this, pieces of a dismembered body could be seen, the torso itself having been chopped into three parts; to his right another head caught his attention, its eyes gouged out and its jaw torn off; and the last of his friends lay disemboweled – Jim was reminded of deer he had seen on the side of the road, eviscerated by tractor-trailers. This was too much. He wanted to run, to move, to do anything but be still, yet that was all he could manage. Then he began to tremble, shaking uncontrollably, and the hooded ghouls or bogeymen or demons or whatever they were turned their attention on him. They reached for their bows, and somehow ignited the tips of the arrows they held by touching them with their distorted, elongated fingers. This done, they set the arrows to the bowstrings and took aim. Jim felt his head go cold and wet.

The arrows were released and sped towards him, towards his rapidly beating heart.

"Mary save me!" he cried. It was more of an instinct than a thought.

At once, the weapons fell short and lay sizzling on the ground. He looked in front of him to see the cloaks slip off the screeching monsters to expose mere skeletons, which crumbled into dust. Then he looked up. The sky, which had been pitch black, was now brilliantly blue with a few cottony clouds to add to its beauty. He also noticed that there was no sun. The source of light appeared to emanate from atop a cloud in the distance, a cloud that was slowly descending toward Jim. As it grew closer, he could see someone standing on it. Although she originally shone brighter than the sun, her radiance seemed to diminish in intensity so he could look upon her.

When she smiled at him he knew who she was. For, she possessed a beauty and a grace which he had never before seen, but which he immediately recognized.

"Remember this moment," she spoke. "You alone pleaded for my help."

Chapter Five

REALITY CHECK

HE TURNED over in his bed. His blankets were on the floor, and his pillow was squeezed between the wall and the mattress. His shorts and t-shirt were uncomfortably clammy. And for a few seconds he remained in limbo between sleeping and waking. Then, fully rousing himself, he sat up and stared at his naked bed, pondering the dream he had just experienced.

"I've been watching too many horror movies," he decided.

Next, he reflected upon his meeting with Kor and concluded that it was entirely possible for their meeting to have been a dream as well. In fact, he was having difficulty distinguishing that day's dream world from the real world. As he continued this mental struggle he used his damp shirt sleeve to wipe the beads of sweat still lingering on his forehead. This simple, almost unconscious motion allowed him to collect his thoughts, and he decided he was no longer in a dream. Not only was he awake, but his mouth was terribly dry. Standing up he lumbered to the kitchen. The lights had been left on, and he wondered if anybody else was awake. After a quick look around he decided that whoever went to bed last had forgotten to turn the lights off. Then he picked up a glass and clumsily filled it with water. As he raised it to his lips, the wet glass slipped through his grip shattering on the tile floor. At first he hoped the loud crash hadn't woken anyone. However, as the seconds passed and nobody stirred, he began thinking something was amiss. According to the clock on the oven, it was three in the morning. True, the rest of his family could have been in a deep sleep, but he doubted it. Trying to ignore the feeling that was creeping over him, he fetched the broom. Slowly, he swept the broken glass into the dustpan. Then, after he was convinced he had sufficiently cleaned the floor, he tested it in a way that would only be done by a teenager at three in the morning – he walked over it in his bare feet. As it turned out, he had not sufficiently cleaned the floor, and a transparent piece of glass sliced into the heel of his left foot. Before he could catch himself, he let out a squeal. It was an effeminate high-pitched scream, muffled after only a second. But it was enough.

When no member of his family responded to the noise, he gave in to his fears and hobbled as fast as he could to his parents' bedroom, leaving bloody prints of his left heel behind him. Opening the door, he found a slightly disheveled bed in an undisturbed room. He made his way to Pauly's room and found it the same. He began yelling for his parents, for his brother, hoping beyond reason that they would jump out from some closet and laughingly shout "Surprise!" When this didn't happen, he hurried outside to check the garage, thinking that, possibly, they could have left in one of the cars. This was far more reasonable, he felt, than thinking they were playing a practical joke on him at three in the morning. But both of the family cars were in the garage. The idea of running inside to call 911 rushed through his mind. It was at this point that he decided to slow down. He sat on the steps, took a few deep breaths, and began wondering if he were still in a dream. This was too unreal. It must be a dream. He limped inside.

After shutting the front door, he locked it. As he did so, he stared at the door handle, certain that he hadn't unlocked it in the first place. Then the phone rang. Jim flinched back, startled by the sound. But when it rang a second time he forgot about the lock and made his way to the telephone. Once there however, he could not force himself to pick up the receiver. He knew that it might be his mom or dad or Pauly on the other end, but an irrational horror slowly possessed him. Answering the phone was not possible. Instead, he stood insecurely staring at it. The phone rang a third and then a fourth time. Eventually the answering machine went on, and he listened anxiously. No message was left.

He picked up and nervously dialed 911, but there was no answer.

His horror peaked when the doorbell rang. Frozen to his spot, he focused on not fainting. At this moment, he realized that it was not a dream. Though the situation resembled a nightmare, there was nothing dreamlike about his ability to reason, nor about the fear welling up within him. He was not going to answer the door. The doorbell rang again. With a Herculean act of the will, he held himself together. Dropping to his hands and knees he crawled toward the basement stairs. It seemed illogical to enter a place with no exit, but he had always felt safe in his basement.

He was halfway down the stairs when he heard the front-door window shatter. He had made it to the bottom when he heard footsteps in the hallway. It would have been less terrifying if someone had called for him, for good or ill. The silent steps that followed the breaking of the window sounded almost hollow, and it was this ghostlike quality that was most unnerving. At least from a voice he could envision what the intruder looked like. But this formless unknown in his mind was the most horrifying thought of all. He could hear the footsteps searching the living room, the kitchen, the dining room... his room. After his room, the steps passed by the basement door and began their slow, hollow thudding upstairs to his parents' room. He could no longer make out where they were taking the intruder, so he began to think of what to do. He was reminded of his grade school days when he would come down to the basement to play "Hun Kanny". This was most likely the reason why the basement felt like a safe haven. Here Hun Kanny had defeated all manner of villainous monsters. During those years, he had saved towns, cities, and countries from the most despicable of creatures.

Jim began remembering some of the games he had played. One time Hun Kanny was on the verge of being defeated by a monster named Kilza. She was a three-headed giant python. As the game progressed, the python body grew six thick, bulky legs, and Hun Kanny was no match for her. She was too strong and too fast. Everything he tried to do was a complete failure, and he had narrowly escaped being shredded to pieces by the mighty jaws of her left head. In the end he decided to try the element of surprise. Hiding in the bulkhead and waiting, he knew she would come by sooner or later. The attack must be timed perfectly. When he heard her enter the wood storage area, he threw open the door, and with one mighty swipe at the back of her neck his forceful blade had removed all three of her heads. This sent her body into a violent flailing of legs and tail that came dangerously close to him, but, with a few quick movements, Hun Kanny was able to dodge the senseless whipping and slashing until it simmered down to a slow writhing of body parts that signaled the end of her treachery.

The bulkhead! He had forgotten that. The basement was divided into two equal halves. Coming down the stairs, to the left was a playroom filled with games, exercise equipment and a large wooden desk. There was a steel support pole off to the left side of the room, which he used to run into when he failed to look where he was going. To the right was the storage area filled with the extra freezer, the tool table, the wood, and the wood-burning stove his family used to heat the house in the winter. They had chords and chords of wood. The greater part of it was in neatly piled stacks in the backyard or in the sides of the garage, but the supply for the coming winter was thrown down the bulkhead and stacked in this storage area near the stove. Most of the time he played in the playroom, but the memory of Kilza brought his attention to the bulkhead, and he stood up to hurry over to the storage room. He had forgotten about his sensitive wound; taking his first step, he put pressure on it and crumpled back down on the ground. This time, he was able to refrain from squealing in pain. Biting his lip, he looked back at the gash in his left heel. The shard of glass which had sliced into his foot had left a few slivers lodged in the cut. Unable to remove them, he crawled to the bulkhead door. As he quietly closed it behind him, he heard the basement door open. Slowly and quietly he made his way up the few stairs to the outer door of the bulkhead. He attempted to open it but forgot to unlatch it first. His heart began to pound heavily again, for he knew that the latch hook held tight to its eye screw and would come out with a loud "pop!" There were no more footsteps to be heard. The basement floor was rug on cement, and the hollow stepping of the intruder ceased to make noise once it left the stairs. Jim realized that in real life Hun Kanny could never have defeated Kilza surprising her from the bulkhead. He would have no way of knowing when to attack.

At this point he heard a bump against the pole in the playroom. He managed a faint smile and quickly popped open the latch, scampered through the opening and ran. The pain in his heel was quite sharp, but he managed to overcome it, sprinting as fast as he could into the forest behind the house, never looking back. The time for thinking was over. Pure adrenaline-fed stamina carried him barefoot on his way. In a mist he saw the mixture of trees, mostly dark in the night, with a few white birches standing out. He saw the little stream, and then the leaf coated hill. Years and years of autumns had covered this forest floor with dead foliage, causing it to be soft and damp. His bare feet felt the cool comfort of these leaves, and it soothed his heel. Once over the hill, however, came the end of the forest, and he was in the open. It all went by so quickly that he was tempted to slow down. But he didn't hesitate. He knew that at the other side of the opening was Central Park, and on the other side of Central Park was the western bank of the river. The hard surface of the street was a sharp contrast to the forest floor, but this was followed by the soft, cushiony grass of the park. He sprinted over the grass and reached the river before he knew why he had run there so frantically. Doubling over, he gasped for breath.

When he was ready, he stood up and thought about the previous morning. He knew that it hadn't been a dream. He had definitely talked with Kor: "Too many people are depending on you. And most of them don't even know it."

He sat on the bank and wept, crying confused and sorrowful tears. There was no way of knowing where his family had gone, but he felt certain that his failure to act earlier that day had everything to do with their disappearance.

The throbbing in his left heel actually helped him regain composure. He knew that an infected heel would lessen his chances of accomplishing anything. So he spent the next few minutes washing the wound with the river water. Then he ripped off a piece of cloth from the bottom of his shirt to act as a bandage. As he tied it around his foot, he chuckled at himself despite the situation, not knowing if this was even the right thing to do. He was wrapping it simply because he had seen people in movies do that.

"But," he reasoned, "it can't make it any worse."

It was some time after three in the morning, so the fact that the town was asleep as he had run through it did not surprise him. But nothing was moving. Not one car was on the busiest road. He sat on the bank and looked upstream at the bridge that connected the east and west sides of the town. Everything was still. Then he was startled to see a cage being pulled toward the bridge. Though he was unable to see what was in it, the entire scene smelled rotten... "sinister" was the word that came to mind. Something forceful, something deep down inside told him he needed to act immediately. He couldn't explain it, but it moved him, and he began hobbling toward the bridge.

Memorial Bridge was at least seventy-five feet above him when he arrived at its base. Looking up he was reminded of the fence that used to span the bridge. It had been erected to prevent the patients of the local mental health institution from jumping off the side to their deaths. Recently the fence had been taken down for renovations, but thus far none of the "lunatics" had tried to fly from its newly open rails. Now, under the bridge, he saw for the first time the true insanity of such a jump. Yet he was going to scale the bridge for the sole purpose of doing just that.

As he struggled up the side of the foundation he tried to push the thought of those who had lunged to their deaths from his mind, but he couldn't succeed. Some of their bodies had been found on the banks of the river; some were found on the riverbed; but some would jump during the spring when the snow from the north had finally melted causing the river to rise, and these bodies were never found. It was assumed that their dead bodies had floated down the river disappearing into the Atlantic Ocean. This was the worst thought of all – never to be found. Sure he would be dead anyway, but something about his body not being found filled him with utter horror. "Of course," he comforted himself, "it isn't spring."

And with that he tried to focus on what he was doing. The taut wires around the support legs were just close enough for him to use as a ladder. Once arriving at the large metal brace under the bridge, he crawled along its bottom lip, trying not to look down to his left, as he hugged the wall of steel to his right. He was forced, however, to look down every so often to see if he had made it to the middle of the river. The feeling of vertigo was strong but, surprisingly, not overwhelming, and he was able to continue on until he made it to his destination.

There he was, on all fours like a cat in a tree. He knew what he had to do, but he couldn't do it.

He began to think of himself as a gargoyle on the side of a building and wondered why he felt that he was so necessary for everyone's salvation. The first thoughts of heading back to safety crept into his mind, but he hadn't forgotten his parents' empty room, his brother's empty room, and so he remained. "If anybody finds my dead body in the river below, they'll think it was suicide." He didn't want to be *the kid who went crazy and killed himself.* Then he thought of the footsteps. Those were real... and so was the cage, and so was Kor. If he didn't fall into the river there might not be anybody to remember him as anything. He convinced himself that it was similar to jumping into the cold lakes of Maine in the summer. There was a certain amount of reckless abandon involved. He would need to jump off a rock and fully immerse his body, or he would never get in for a swim. But still, he would be tentative, fearing the shock of the icy water. "In the end, though, I always jump."

With that thought, he hung off the side of the brace, holding on with his hands just long enough to say a prayer. Then he let go.

HE FELT his stomach rise to his throat and tried to maintain his pencil-like position. He knew a belly flop from this height would kill him. "This is definitely not a dream," he thought as his body accelerated toward the water and broke through.

His feet hit the riverbed. His legs should have snapped like toothpicks, followed by his spine, followed by death. But his feet continued, as if entering a sponge. He decelerated as his entire body was consumed in a soft, cushiony muck. Expecting to come to a complete halt, he instead passed through his doorway into water. Losing his sense of equilibrium, he began kicking and thrashing in a panic, but then, regaining his wits, he relaxed and allowed himself to float to the surface.

PART II

LUKE'S JOURNEY

Even were I to walk in a ravine as dark as death
I should fear no danger, for you are at my side.
Your staff and your crook are there to soothe me.

You prepare a table for me
Under the eyes of my enemies;
You anoint my head with oil;
My cup brims over.
(Psalm 23:4-5)

Chapter Six

FRUSTRATION

IT WAS approaching one A.M. on a clear September night when Luke exited the forest and crossed the town line entering Stackingsdale, Maine. Water dripped from his clothes, but he didn't appear to notice. His mission was too important to be bothered by such trivial matters. He knew what he had to do, and he managed to quell a twinge of resentment toward Jim. "Somehow," he reminded himself, "this is all providential... somehow... and I've just got to do my best." The sad truth was that most of the people in the town were doomed to captivity. There was nothing he could do about that now; his sole purpose was to find Jim.

The dragons had never attempted an attack like this before, but the success they had managed that day had made it possible for a crossover into Maine. As he walked down Western Avenue watching the few cars still out after midnight, he was tempted to warn them of the coming peril, but he knew it would be futile. They wouldn't believe him before it happened, and afterward it would be too late. No, he needed to keep to his purpose.

****

THE DAY Luke had just lived through seemed straight from the Book of Job. It was one dreadful event after another. While he had been enjoying breakfast with his brother Kor and a good friend named Vort, a servant rushed in holding a note, which he promptly handed to Kor. After reading the note Kor left abruptly. He told Luke and Vort to wait until he came back, but that was all.

Then a couple of hours later Kor returned with the discouraging news of Jim's refusal, and the other two finally learned what was happening. Hun Kanny, a powerful schwah, was desperately needed. Why and where he was needed was unclear, but it appeared to revolve around dragons. Kor didn't know the specifics; obviously the note had been written in a hurry. The urgency, however, was in no way ambiguous. And the boy, Jim Staving, was the only one who could call Hun Kanny for help. Hives, the writer of the note, had included essential information Kor would need to use to convince Jim.

That conversation, Kor told them, had been one of the most difficult he had ever had. Telling Jim everything would have surely lost him, but not telling him enough had obviously resulted in failure as well. "I *did* tell him that I lived with Impids," he explained, "but did *not* say I was crowned king two years ago. A fifteen-year-old king is a bit much for most non-Impids to accept... but maybe, if I had told him, he would've listened."

"No," Luke comforted him, "no, he wouldn't."

Kor thought it over. "You're right," he agreed. "It wouldn't have made a difference." Then he drummed his fingers on the table, wishing he knew what to do next. "Did Mom and Dad say when they'd be back?" he asked.

"I don't think so," said Luke, knowing why Kor had asked the question. "They didn't want to be stuck to a schedule. Remember?"

Before Kor could respond, Hives came in followed by three Impids. Kor immediately told him that Jim had refused to go. The schwah grabbed a piece of paper and began writing feverishly. He would try to clarify everything that had been happening. He first wrote to apologize for not coming himself that morning, but many things had occurred, troublesome things that were snowballing out of control. He wrote of a place called Calapanta. Until this morning, the doorway connecting the Amazon to Calapanta had been undiscovered. However, about dawn several miles from the palace, acres of jungle mysteriously ignited. When Hives went to put out the fires and to see what had caused them, he quickly discovered the answer. Scribbling down this morning's note to Kor, he handed it to an Impid and then focused on damage control. A dragon was on the other side of the doorway. Although it had not broken through, it had destroyed much of the surrounding area before Hives finally secured the door.

Hives quickly understood that this must be the secret doorway to Calapanta. Before this morning he hadn't thought a dragon, or any schwah, could break through a doorway. But now he saw that, given enough time, a dragon could, in fact, create sufficient pressure to burst through. This disturbance, however, should cause the doorway eventually to disintegrate. Then nobody would be able to cross it, and the dragon would be no better off. Unless... (Here, Hives stopped writing. This newest thought appeared to disturb him greatly. And when he started writing again, he took a different track.) For a dragon to have the time it needed, the situation on the other side must be dire indeed.

Hun Kanny was supposed to protect the land of Calapanta. But he had been silent for several years, having fallen into the deep slumber of a forgotten schwah. Recently he had been crying out in his sleep, crying out to Jim with a jealous yearning. The broken silence had not gone by Hives undetected. And so, when the events transpired that morning, Hives thought of Jim. He had hoped that Jim would listen to Kor, and that the true guardian of Calapanta would awaken to defeat the dragon. But Jim refused. A much riskier road must now be taken, for they needed to find out what was happening in Calapanta. To do this, someone would have to sneak through the very doorway the dragon had attempted to destroy.

It would be a treacherous mission. They all knew that. Getting in would be the easy part. It was returning that would be difficult. And when the decision was made, they chose Vort. Vort was not only a good friend and a top aide to Kor, but he was also one of the smaller and craftier Impids. And he had volunteered immediately. It was the right choice.

Vort left and was gone for hours. As time ticked by, Kor was tempted to go through, fearing for Vort's life. Hives held him back, however, reminding him to have patience. This was not something that could be accomplished quickly.

When Vort finally returned, their relief was short lived, for he bore disheartening news. There were three dragons in Calapanta, and they had discovered the mapping for the doorways throughout the land. In less than a week, the defenders of Calapanta had been forced to the country's outskirts.

Vort didn't learn how the dragons came to be free in the first place, but such was the present state of affairs: The dragons had called out the clungens and were preparing to send them through the doorway to Maine. This move was predictable. The clungens were the dragons' slaves, their ghouls – people they had captured and tortured into submission. No longer human, they had given up all hope, and in their hateful despair would do the dragons' bidding, driven on by an envy of all who remained free. It made perfect sense that they would be sent to capture more slaves.

And the sleepy town of Stackingsdale would be completely helpless. Just as dragons are unaffected by any weapon untouched by a schwah, so their slaves, once stripped of their humanity, are beyond the reach of such weapons as well. The struggle would be short. Then with Stackingsdale conquered, the dragons themselves could be let through. The town would serve as the launch pad for future attacks on surrounding cities. They would expand their dominion, turning the humans into more ghoulish slaves. The dragons planned to become so powerful that no schwah could possibly defeat them.

Then, as Vort was still speaking, the doorway to the Amazon spouted a burst of flame. At least one of the dragons had detected the breach. The next several hours were spent defending the doorway. Though the battle resulted in no loss of life, they did lose much precious time. When the struggle finally ended and the dragon was turned away, it was night. They needed to act at once.

Kor and Luke could not afford to wait for their parents. They were miles away exploring in the jungle, and, as Luke had reminded Kor, it was uncertain as to when they would return. This was the first such expedition their father had taken with their mother since the freakish accident that had crippled his left leg. For two years he had flatly refused to venture into the jungle again. It was only recently that he had even considered it. So, when he surprised their mother last week, saying he would go, she was overjoyed. And as they prepared to leave, they were quite clear about their intentions. The two were planning on thoroughly enjoying themselves; they might not be back for days.

Kor would have to do without their advice. He regretted this but quickly gathered his council. Soon he was sitting with Hives and his top Impids discussing the present situation.

Kor's initial thought had been to go to Maine himself, but Luke had strongly objected to this. It was unwise, he argued, for Kor to leave the Amazon at the moment. Given the feeble state of the doorway protecting them from the dragons, it was essential that the king's subjects remain his first priority. Hives agreed. So this idea was promptly discarded. Sending Hives himself was not an option because the only door he could use to enter Maine had been closed two years ago. Kor's next idea was to send Vort, who had proven himself worthy in his previous mission that day. Luke, once again, disagreed: Asking Vort to risk his life twice in the same day when there were other options was not just... anyway, he continued, it would be more reasonable to send someone who knew Maine. That left only one person.

Luke was Kor's most trusted aide, but he was also his younger brother... "Sending me," Luke persuaded, "would be almost like going yourself. It's the right choice." Again, Hives agreed.

Luke was given some last minute instructions. He was told how he would know when the clungens had broken through the doorway from Calapanta into Maine. It would be best if he could find Jim before this occurred, but if he couldn't, he would have to take care not to be noticed. However, he *must* find Jim. It would be quite easy to hide through the beginning of the attack. The clungens, depending on the element of surprise, would be capturing as many people as possible, not expecting anyone to hide from them. If he had already found Jim by this time, the two of them could possibly make it back to the Amazon undetected. If not, a more forbidding path lay ahead. He would know that the initial stage was ending when he heard the telephones ringing. The clungens would be calling to rouse any who had slept through the first strike. They would then struggle with the more difficult cases. "And," he was told, "No matter how bad it looks, Hun Kanny is sure to make Jim a 'more difficult case'." How Hun Kanny would do this was unknown, but that it would be done was not doubted. Also, Luke mustn't let down his guard should it appear that the attack had ended, especially if Jim's house looked untouched. The dragons' slaves would erase any signs of a struggle. They were sure to do this... the town of Stackingsdale would look peacefully empty by the time they were finished.

Hives reiterated his caution for silence: *Walk softly and speak only in whispers.* Then, when he wrote his last sentence, he underlined it emphatically: ***Make no sound once they are there***!

After he had finished writing, he handed Luke the instructions, and as they made eye contact, Luke noticed a deep sadness hiding behind the schwah's confident eyes, a sadness he had never seen before, not even during the Seeker Wars that had decimated the Impids for over twelve years. Luke wanted to ask the reason, but there was no time. He had to leave.

Kor accompanied Luke to the doorway. "Luke, I know this is ultimately my decision," he said, "But I don't like it, Luke. I don't like it at all."

"I know, you'd rather go yourself," interrupted Luke.

"Yes, but that's not it... I don't know... Something bad's going on... something really bad, and," he paused for a moment, "I don't know if you're coming back." His eyes began to tear.

"Kor, I don't know either. This isn't like our other adventures, is it? We've been in trouble before but... I know what you mean." Then they continued walking in silence until they reached the doorway.

"I've gotta go now," said Luke looking up at Kor. "According to Hives, it sounds like I'm in a bit of a hurry."

"Yeah, I know." Kor wiped the tears that had started to flow down his cheeks. Then he hugged Luke, and whispered in his ear, "May the angels be with you, never leaving your side."

A glint shown in Luke's eyes and a smile crossed his face. "Now you sound like Mom," he chuckled.

"Well, I figured she wasn't here to do it," Kor laughed through his tears, "Come on, I'm trying to say goodbye." Then, growing serious, he looked into Luke's eyes, "Mom's right you know," he said. They hugged again; this time silently. And with that Luke passed through the doorway to Stackingsdale, Maine.

****

WHEN HE was halfway down State Street, he saw a great streak of lightning rend the night sky. It was soon followed by a loud, forceful "boom" that shook the ground beneath his feet. The reverberations echoed to the core of his being. The clungens were breaking through. He knew what would happen next. Out would come the people, shocked by the mighty blast, curious as to what had caused it. And they would be met by a ghastly nightmare.

Luke slipped into the woods, slowly, quietly making his way to Jim's house. He heard the clamor of the people being sucked into the cages that the clungens had brought with them, but he remained hidden. At times he was forced to creep near a neighborhood of houses and could hear the telephones ringing. The muffled screams that followed told him that the phones were being answered, that new victims were being captured. Then, as he approached his destination, the terror seemed to come to an abrupt end; stage one was over.

Soon he was standing amongst the last line of trees, looking across the grass towards Jim's house. He had been told exactly where it would be. Then he saw Jim himself limping up the front stairs back into his house.

"Hun Kanny did it!" he thought. Jim had been protected, and this gave Luke a burst of confidence. Now it was time for contact, but as he stepped out from the woods onto the grass he remembered the warning Hives had given him. He must be careful not to be seen or heard. He mustn't let "their" silence fool him. Then he heard the phone ring. He heard it ring a second time and wanted to scream out "Don't pick it up!" He remained silent. It rang four times without being answered. Again, Jim had been protected.

As Luke sidled up the stairs and hid in the shadows of the front porch, he thought about the risk he now needed to take. If Jim would answer the door, then they could sneak out through the woods before the clungens knew they were there. But to get Jim to answer he needed to ring the doorbell. It would be quieter than knocking. He rang it once and noticed that he could barely hear it from the outside. This was good, but Jim didn't answer. He rang it again, and there was still no answer. The urgency of the situation took its toll on Luke, and he pressed his elbow against the lower right window pane hoping it would give way silently. It didn't. The broken glass shattered on the floor. Quickly he reached in, and unlocked the door. He knew he couldn't call for Jim. After the breaking glass, any more noise would be a death wish. Unnerved, he breathlessly made his way to the living room. In his mind's eye, he could clearly see the thick, underlined letters of the last directive Hives had given him, and he attempted to hide. But then, before finding an adequate hiding place, he remembered the first directive: he *must* find Jim. No clungens had entered the house, and he began thinking the noise of the breaking window had been amplified by his nervous ears. So he left the living room to search the dining room and then the bedroom across the hall. The bedroom was in disarray: the bedspread undone, the blankets strewn about the floor, and the pillow wedged between the mattress and the wall. Jim was nowhere to be found.

Finally, he returned to the kitchen. This time he noticed the bloody heal prints on the floor. He followed them up the stairs to the master bedroom. Finding it empty, he walked down the hall, passed the bathroom, and entered another bedroom; it was empty as well. As he stood there wondering what to do next, it struck him that if these bloody marks were Jim's then there might have already been some manner of struggle that set Jim on his guard. This would account for him not answering the door. Luke then thought of the basement. It probably had many places to hide.

Down he went, slowly, for he didn't want to make any more noise than necessary. When he reached the bottom, he had a choice to make – right or left. He turned left. The room was almost pitch-black, but he could just make out the obstacles in his way. Dodging one of them, he smacked his head against the metal pole. This not only surprised him but also caused him to lose his balance, and he fell to the ground. He was slightly shaken when he heard an indistinct snapping sound from the other side of the basement, followed by a quick bang of a door being opened. Then all was silent. He reached for the pole and hoisted himself back on his feet. As he walked to the other side of the basement, a slight chill ran down his spine. He didn't know if the sound had been someone leaving or someone entering. Regaining his courage, he reminded himself that everything would turn out fine if he simply did what he needed to do.

Entering the storage area, he located the bulkhead door. With another burst of courage, he opened it. Finding the outer door ajar, he climbed the stairs and went out into the night.

Chapter Seven

CAPTURED!

HE SHOULD have been more careful. He knew that. In his desire to find Jim as quickly as possible he ran straight through the backyard, forgetting, if just for a moment, the extreme danger of the situation. One step after entering the forest, however, he paused. Something didn't feel right, and he realized he had made a dire mistake. He could sense eyes watching him... evil eyes that made his hair stand on end. He thought of turning to face them but instead continued on his way, this time more carefully, while trying to overcome the feeling of being watched. But the shadows made this difficult to do. They were moving in an odd manner and appeared to be following him.

Then he ran. The shadows had been growing closer, and he knew that flight was his only chance of escape. It was a reasonable decision, for he was a fast runner. But he was unfamiliar with the terrain. When his left foot kicked against a stump, he tried to maintain his balance with his right, but it landed in a rut, and he tumbled to the ground. Before he could get up, it happened. First he felt the lifeless grip of the skeletal hand on his shoulder. As his blood ran cold he was thrust face down back onto the ground. He was stripped of his sword, and his hands and feet were quickly bound. Then his hooded captor hoisted him over its shoulder, throwing the sword carelessly into a thicket beside them. Luke thought back to the last conversation he had had with Kor, to the feeling neither of them could express, but which both of them had felt, and the full weight of his error came crashing down on him. Hives could not have been more adamant. And now he was being carried like a sack of potatoes out of the forest, where a second clungen joined them.

The one carrying him turned to the other and grumbled, "That's all of them." Even though Luke was frozen with fear, he knew the importance of that statement, the vital importance of the meaning it conveyed. They thought he was the last remaining resident of the house. He remembered something else Hives had written... *never give up*. In one aspect the plan had succeeded – Jim had escaped!

This thought failed to comfort him for long, however, for he knew what was coming: Torture. He knew as well that he was too weak to bear it alone, so he prayed for the strength he needed to resist... to resist the despair of which Hives had warned him. The clungens had an insatiable hunger for despair. And they would punish him until he gave up all hope, until he became one of them.

The two clungens appeared to be in no hurry. As they slowly stomped through the backyard and between the house and garage, Luke began to wonder how he could possibly escape, bound as he was. He remembered close calls in enemy castles. This was not the first time he had been captured either. But, in those other instances, there had always been an Impid ready to risk life and limb to save him. Sometimes it was Kor himself. Sometimes it was their father. This time, it appeared, he had been the one to do the saving, and now he was alone.

The clungen threw him to the ground. Then came fear – the real fear. His body was gripped in terror as he beheld the cage being rolled down the street. He could hear the dismal moans of the captives within, for that was all they could manage. Screams, wails, pleas for mercy – these would have been less terrifying than the barely audible sounds that reached his ears. No, this mournful groaning merely intensified the dreadful spectacle confronting him. And his stomach knotted into a painful nausea. Several wooden posts had been erected down the center of the large forty-foot long cage. Each prisoner had not merely been locked up, but, above his head, his wrists had been nailed to the post. No room was wasted. The poor captives were impaled to the wood, one on top of the other, so that the lowest layer of humans was lying across the bottom of the cage. Slightly above them, another layer was affixed, and so on and so forth, until the top layer was standing on those beneath, arms extended high above them. This was done on the four sides of every post. And each captive was facing out so that Luke could see the silent horror on the contorted faces of those too overwhelmed to cry out. At first he retched; then he turned his head to vomit but failed to clear his shirt. He looked back at the two clungens who had brought him here; they were unmoved.

They opened the gate, and Luke was thrown in. The revolting stench of his shirt soon disappeared, or, rather, melded with the foul reek inside the cage. He was not the only one who couldn't stomach the sight he had beheld; the mixture of body odor and vomit, combined with the rot of the clungens themselves was suffocating. There were several clungens inside keeping watch. One of these grabbed Luke by the arms and, without untying him, pressed his wrists to a post. He saw the spike it held in its hand and was tempted to struggle. He was tempted to yell out, to scream, to wail for mercy, but he resisted all these temptations. He felt the sharp point touch his right wrist, and bowing his head, he squeezed his eyes shut.

Then, as the hammer sounded, his head shot up, and he pierced the sky with an agonizing stare that beckoned Heaven above for deliverance. His mouth opened, and he emitted a groan emerging from the depths of his soul, yet it failed to help. There was nothing he could do to match the pain. His eyes rolled back in his head, and he dropped his chin to his chest as he lost consciousness. Thus, pinned to a wooden post, hanging above a packed cage of humanity, he was rolled down Sewell Street to the local high school.

****

WHEN HE awoke, he was sitting on the floor of a dark classroom with his back against the wall and his arms stretched above him. Once again, he was alone. His hands and feet were still tied, and his legs had gone numb. He no longer had a nail through his wrists, but they were burning from the wound; on fire it seemed, a fire that increased in intensity with the slightest movement. Slipping through the ropes would not be possible. He was too tightly bound, or at least that's what he imagined. Any attempt to pull free was met with an unbearably excruciating pain. And squirming across the floor was not possible either, as his hands were somehow mounted to the wall. He tried to discover what held them fast, but when he looked up, the wall itself prevented him from bending his neck to see them.

Staring straight ahead, he could just make out a massive chain in the far corner of the room. Each of its great iron links looked to be roughly half a foot in diameter, and leaning against the wall next to them were several thick metal plates. Other than the chain and those plates, the room was empty – no desks, no shelves, no books.

Then the clungen entered. Its hood hid its features, but he could clearly see its blood-red eyes. Its charcoal cloak completely covered its limbs. A short, balding man followed it in and turned on the light. The man appeared to be in his fifties and was wearing a navy blue suit with white dress shirt and black wingtip shoes. Looking through his spectacles at Luke, he smiled with a twinkle in his eyes. Then he spoke:

"Let me begin by telling you that I am overjoyed everything has gone so well. I did not expect to be able to come over so soon. Of course I should not be surprised at the pragmatism of your fellow Mainahs," he said, imitating their accent. "Your choice is simple: the first option is to join us and be brought to the rooftop to be taken back to our land; the second option is for us to 'encourage' you, so to speak, to choose the first option." Here he paused for a moment, looked out the window, and then continued. "From what I understand, your wrists must be smarting a bit. It really is a shame; unfortunately, my workers don't care much for stragglers. If you had come out when we first called you, you would have found your trip much more comfortable. But not to worry, we have something that takes care of the pain in seconds... better than aspirin." He winked at Luke. "All you have to do is ask."

Luke remained silent. He knew he lacked the strength to give the courageous answer – after all, the old man was right; his wrists *did* hurt – but he also refused to give in.

"So many of your compatriots have already chosen the first option that I'm really quite impressed. Such wisdom and prudence is truly edifying. But if you do decide to remain obstinate, we will, of course, dabble with some additional physical torture," he continued, "but would like to concentrate on the mental torment that Luntha, here, enjoys much more. Unfortunately, thus far, not a one has survived the merely mundane 'encouragements'. Isn't that right Luntha?"

Here, Luke's eyes twitched toward the chain.

This reaction did not go by the old man unnoticed. "You mustn't fret over that," he said. "*That* is for someone who has not shown up quite yet." Here he puckered his lips, and clicked his tongue in mock disappointment.

"As for you, my dear, we have something different in mind if *you* fail to cooperate."

Luke again refused to speak. Luntha continued to remain still – a statue, glaring at Luke with its beady, red eyes. And the short man in the suit began strolling around the room. He made two full circuits, then said, "Well, Luntha, what do you think? Does silence mean consent?" Luntha did not answer. "No, no, I guess not. We don't want to bring a traitor back accidentally do we? I guess we had better make sure he's with us... Well, I suppose it's time to free him from the wall. Luntha, would you be so kind as to remove the nail from his hands."

Luke was shocked, not that they would nail his hands to the wall; no, he expected that kind of treatment. Rather, he was shocked that there could be a nail driven through the palms of his hands, and he wouldn't know it. When his bound hands fell onto his lap, he looked at them as though they were foreign, not part of his body – as if toy, plastic hands from a mannequin had somehow been attached to his burning wrists. He was mesmerized by the four nail holes, and stared at them intensely. The blood was still flowing smoothly from the holes in his hands. The bespectacled man noticed the attention he was giving his wounds: "Ah, yes. I see you're curious about the separate nail holes. It wouldn't do to use the same hole twice... much too difficult, the nail head might slip through the opening, you know." Then he sauntered toward the door, leaned over, whispered something in Luntha's ear, and left.

Luntha moved toward Luke. Slowly it unsheathed its weapon. It raised its arm, and Luke could see the long, bloodstained blade it held from under the cloak. He knew the thing would not kill him, for that would not be torture. But he could not imagine how it was about to use the weapon. The suspense itself was torturous. Then it slashed straight down, and he thought the creature was cutting his hands off. But to his immense surprise, his hands fell freely to his sides. The clungen made its way to his feet and slashed again. This time, Luke was sure he was losing his feet at the ankles, but, as with his hands, only the bonds were cut.

Before, Luke was unable to speak due to pure dread. Now, it was confusion that held his tongue. He looked up to see the creature move a human finger in front of its face, making a sign for Luke to remain silent. He could not believe it. Somebody – he knew not who – had managed to save him. At least that's what he thought. This was a bit later than he would have hoped, but somehow they had done it! His legs were numb making it difficult to stand, and the fire that burned in his wrists was unbearable, but none of that mattered. He was free... or almost free.

Luntha pointed to the door, motioning to Luke. Luke, believing he was being asked to open it, obediently attempted to turn the handle. His numb fingers could not grip, however, and the pain in his wrist was too much. He managed to press his knuckles weakly against the door handle, but that was all. His hands were of no use. He turned to ask Luntha for help, but Luntha had already reached around and opened the door. Then the point of the knife was pressed between his shoulder blades. Luke was startled at first, but when the knife did no more than urge him forward, he quickly deduced what must be happening. He was to follow where that point led him, pretending to be a horror-stricken prisoner, until this savior of his led him down the stairs, out of the school, and away from the other clungens.

The point did not lead him down the stairs. Rather, he found himself walking upstairs. And as the point led him to the rooftop he began to question himself. He could not see how going into Calapanta with the other prisoners would help him escape. Then he began to ask himself other questions. "Who was that little bald man? And what did he whisper to

Luntha?" But the point continued to lead him, and the questions remained unanswered. It led him to the opening between the worlds, then through the doorway and into Calapanta.

As he stood in this new and unfamiliar land, he saw yet another large, wheeled cage in front of him. He stepped toward its open gate. But, before he could enter, his captor, or redeemer – Luke couldn't decide which it was – leaned close to his ear and whispered, "Fall on your knees and close your eyes."

Luke fell to his knees, clapping his eyes shut. He heard the gate close in front of him. Then came the creak of the wheels as the cage was dragged off he knew not where, and the two of them were left alone. He turned around to face the person who had freed him. No one was there.

Chapter Eight

PSALM 91

IS NOT ALWAYS WHAT IT SEEMS

LUKE WAS experienced enough to know that conclusions derived under extreme stress could sometimes be quite wrong. So he decided to take it slowly, and clear his mind of the recent horror. This was difficult to do, for the pain in his wrists continued to throb intensely. Taking a deep breath, he absorbed his surroundings.

Dawn was fast approaching, allowing him to see into the distance. The surrounding area was devoid of life. He was standing on dry, broken earth – scorched by the hot rays of the sun. It was obvious that no rain had fallen for months. The broken crust was speckled with boulders of diverse shapes and sizes extending out to the line of mountains several miles away.

If he remained in the desert he was sure to die, so he began walking toward the mountains – walking and thinking.

"I was probably wrong about that human clungen who freed me," he thought. "Maybe *this* is what that old man whispered to him... Why would they do this?" He was walking past the boulders, squinting to see the mountains. "He comes in pretending to torture me, then tells the clungen to bring me to Calapanta and leave me alone..." He stopped here and wondered whether to continue this line of reasoning, or to reconsider. "Maybe the human clungen fooled the guy with the glasses... or maybe it was a test, and the guy with the glasses snuck in to save me, and this was the best he could do... yeah that's it!" He thought he had hit upon something here. "That's it! How else could they get me here, fooling all the other clungens. They couldn't let me know, or else I might give it away."

Luke continued more quickly now; even with the constant pain, his heart felt lighter. But it wasn't ten minutes before he halted:

"No... that makes no sense. Ahhhh – this is crazy!" He groaned out loud. "It doesn't explain the cage leaving me here just because I fell on my knees and closed my eyes. No... no..." and he began pondering his first line of reasoning again. "Where did he go? He was behind me, not in front of me. I felt the knife touching my back until I dropped to my knees. The cage left before he got on... I know it. That means he's here somewhere. Why would he be here spying on me?"

This confused Luke for quite some time. But time, it seemed, was a luxury Luke had at the moment. He had been rushing all night, and now he was lost, walking toward mountains, not really knowing why, convinced he was being watched by someone, and the someone who was watching him was apparently content to hide behind a boulder somewhere.

He was on the verge of yelling out, telling the clungen that he knew he was being watched. But, just before he did, the obvious hit him: They didn't know he was Luke. They thought he was Jim. "And if I tell them that I know what they're doing, it might spoil their mistake."

This gave Luke a new line of reasoning: "Now why would they leave Jim here just to watch him walk toward the mountains?" He had no answer but continued walking toward those mountains. For some reason that's what he thought Jim would do. But he was too exhausted, and it took too much concentration to overcome the pain. Slowly he came to a halt.

"There might be more than one," he thought, "There might be a pair of eyes watching me from every vantage point. I need to act relieved and excited that I somehow escaped more torture." He tried again to act as though he were Jim. Slowly, he picked up his step. Once again, however, his wounds were making any act of joy difficult, also, those watching might grow suspicious if a teenager with pierced wrists skipped his way toward unknown mountains.

Two realizations struck him at that moment: first that he was not capable of thinking straight, not for very long at any rate – this was obvious from his behavior; and second, that time was not on his side. He had been thinking so much about his situation, trying to block out the pain in his wrists, that he had utterly forgotten about his pierced hands – they were swollen, infected, and they needed medical attention soon. He picked up his pace a touch, this time with a sense of urgency. The distinct possibility that he could die here in the desert now urged him on.

"I have to pretend that I think I'm alone until I make it to the mountains. After I get there, I don't know. But I need to find help somehow. Somewhere around here there are people willing to help me. I won't believe... I can't believe that the dragons have defeated everyone. I can't believe that." Such were his thoughts. Then he whispered to himself, "Don't give up, Luke."

He decided he would attempt his escape one goal at a time: Goal number one – those mountains. So he continued, believing he was being watched, but with no actual evidence of the fact. He tried to take in his surroundings without looking around too much. He never looked behind him, not wanting to give them any reason to grow suspicious. But focusing intently on what was in front, he tried to keep a map in his mind of the boulders he had passed. This became tedious after a short period of time. He had to keep bringing himself back from one distraction or another.

Then came the heat. As the sun continued its climb, it brought a heat Luke had never felt before. The Amazon would get hot at times, but there was always cover, always shade. Here there was no recourse. He had no hat to protect his face or his neck. His t-shirt protected his upper arms, and his shorts, his upper legs. He pondered removing his green shirt and wrapping it around his head, but decided he would rather burn his face and neck than his back and chest. Keeping his focus was growing increasingly difficult:

"It's hot! Hot, hot, hot! Too hot... boulders, yes, remember boulders. Where are they? Being followed... being watched... It's hot – I'm burning up. This has got to be hotter than the Sahara... than Death Valley. I feel like I'm in a car, and somebody forgot to roll down the windows... There's a boulder – got to remember that one, big one, big enough to hind behide... I'm getting dizzy... it's hot... my wrists hurt."

He could see his arms were already pink, and imagined what his face must look like. Every once in a while he reminded himself why he was enduring this torment. But each time he concluded that he did not know what had happened to Jim, and could not think clearly enough to figure it out. He even had to remind himself that he *was* being watched. The temptation to doubt this would come over him quite strongly at times, but he would not allow himself to give in. It was the only thing that made sense when he could think fairly straight, so he refused to trust himself now that the sun was draining him.

And the sun *was* draining him. The infection in his numb hands was slowly running up his arms, and spots buzzed around in front of his eyes. His legs were losing their feeling as well. Slowly he felt himself slipping. He dropped to his knees, but this time unintentionally. Just as he was about to fall face forward onto the burnt earth he shot out his numbed hands and stopped himself. The pain, which flamed up from his wrists the moment his fists hit the ground, penetrated his entire body. He began to shake violently, feeling as though his arms were too frail to support his upper body, but he must not give in now. It would be so easy to lose consciousness again – so easy to faint away... but he knew that in this heat it would mean death. He argued with himself over this point. It was indeed tempting to rest for just a little while. Then when he came back he would be strong enough to finish the struggle.

The truth prevailed. The tremendous pain passing through his body cleared his head, so he could see this truth: he would die if he fainted. It was a brief lucid moment, but it allowed him to think straight. He needed to continue. He must go on.

Then, with this decision made, he began seeing something else clearly as well. In his struggle to stand, to fight the pain and continue walking, something preternatural occurred. He could see someone else struggling for survival, someone distant. Although the vision was merely an obscure shadow, he knew it was Jim. And although he couldn't tell what the struggle was, he could feel Jim's need as intensely as he felt the burning fire in his wrists... "Jim, don't give up," he thought, "hold on." Then he opened his mouth to yell, to bellow out encouragement; and all he could manage was a whisper: "I'm holding on for you!" His lips barely moved, and the phrase died out inaudibly. But in his heart it boomed. It boomed across the ocean. And Luke slowly, but resolutely, rose to his feet.

****

"CLUNGENS, CLUNGENS all around... but not a drop to drink." Thirst. The sun cooked his lips, but thirst swelled his tongue. It stuck to the bottom of his mouth, to the roof, to his cheeks. Sometimes, when he swallowed, he felt as if he would rip the very skin from his throat. Luke had been praying in the depths of his soul since the beginning of this wretched journey, praying for relief, for release from this inhuman travail. But now the prayer rose to the forefront. It consumed him: "God, give me water!" he pleaded, and he feebly kicked a boulder, hoping for a miracle... none was forthcoming. He *must* forget his thirst if he were to survive. If he kept going, he would make it to the mountains. He would arrive at his goal before this defeated him. He needed to distract himself from the maddening thirst. And kicking boulders was not the way to do it. Focusing on the passing landscape was tiresome as well; he needed to fight to maintain consciousness, and he needed to forget his thirst. Finally, he gave up on memorizing the terrain. He decided to put one foot in front of the other and follow where his mind took him...

****

THERE THEY were - the four of them celebrating their first meal together in the Amazon. As they prepared to eat, Luke stared out at the horizon watching the sun set. He had long known that this was not the Amazon he had learned about in school. The breeze which bathed them would not have been possible in that humid place from his school books. No, this was a marvelously beautiful Amazon, and as the family prepared to dine in the gloaming of the day, he was struck with its magnificent splendor. In fact, he thought, this was far too pleasant an evening for any earthly place at all.

And then there was the meal itself. It was simple, but perfect in every way. The table at which they sat was decked with exotic fruits, but it was the watermelon that stood out... it was easily the juiciest, sweetest melon he had ever had. This refreshing appetizer was followed by a main course of venison.

Luke had never had venison before; he enjoyed it very much. But the taste of the food was not what he remembered most. It was the love. Love saturated and perfected the evening. They consumed the love that night more ravenously than any food. His family was together for the first time... alone. They drank in the love; they celebrated the love with food, with jokes, with stories. Luke could not remember being this happy before. He was content to sit at that table, seeing the look his mom gave his dad, seeing Kor laugh. It was wonderful to be there.

Never much of a talker, Luke soaked it in. He remembered the tears flowing down his cheeks, and not needing to say that there was nothing wrong, because everyone there knew why he was crying. Each member of the family cried similar tears that evening. They had survived together, reunited after years of pain. And it was not until this meal that they could let down their guard. It truly was good to be there.

Then dessert ended, and it was time for bed. He remembered the minutest details of that night. There were no clocks in the palace, no one wore a watch, but it must have been ten or eleven o'clock when he lay down on top of his blankets. Enjoying the comfort of the cool night air, he didn't go to sleep until dawn. He stayed awake remembering his real mom and dad, talking to them for the first time since they had passed away, killed by the emperor during the Seeker Wars when Luke was just a baby. They didn't answer, but he didn't need them to. And he thanked them for the parents who had adopted him, for their friendship with his adoptive father. He thanked them for his very life before finally drifting into a peaceful slumber. He had never bathed in Love as he did that night. That Love, he thought, would help him through anything... then he looked at his hands –

****

THEY WERE massive, almost to the point of rupturing. The wounds closed on themselves; he could just see the puncture festering beneath the swelling. They had made his hands utterly useless. He could tell that the infection was continuing to spread, and he needed help soon. Then he looked at his wrists. They weren't faring much better; the pain had not diminished with the passage of time. The fire continued to burn. In a way, he thanked the burning in his wrists, for it had kept him alive.

When he looked up from these thoughts, he was at the base of the mountains. And it was there, standing only ten feet from shade, that he finally put it all together:

"They think I'm Jim, but Jim doesn't know what I know... They're expecting me to call for Hun Kanny – for the protector of Calapanta. He may be asleep, or lost, or wherever, but they can't really win until they've beaten him. They need him to come into *their* barren wasteland, where all three dragons can attack him together. The cowards would be too frightened to do it any other way; here, he wouldn't stand a chance, and they know he'd go anywhere to save Jim."

He had to think carefully about his next move. If they were watching him, as he expected, then they were not about to let him walk to safety. They would attack as soon as he took his first step on that upslope, expecting him to call for Hun Kanny. No doubt the clungens would attack first, and the dragons would lie in wait until Hun Kanny came. They would want to surprise the schwah to kill him quickly... Then again, they could continue to wait. He might just be able to start his climb, as they waited for him to call to Jim's guardian for salvation. After all, the base of the mountain was nowhere near an escape.

So he stepped. It was just a little step, but it was up more than forward, and he looked upon the thing he had intended to climb. For the first time he truly saw the obstacle that was staring down at him. It was not a hill; it was a mountain. The goal of reaching the base suddenly seemed inadequate. Directly above him, it became steeper. He would have to climb, using his hands to pull his body up. This was, of course, impossible. So, he decided upon a more sideways approach. He would attempt to zigzag his way up.

He commenced mounting the incline, fully expecting to make it to the top. It was steeper and taller than it had looked from the distance, but he had already made it further than he had originally expected, so, he thought, he could finish the task. The sun was illuminating the horizon, and would soon be gone – heat was no longer an issue. Hope began building in him as he hobbled across the side of the mountain.

Then he saw it... or him. Out of the corner of his eye, he was sure he spied movement from behind a boulder at the base. It was no more than thirty feet away. And a new thought dawned on him. They were waiting for him to give up... or die. They brought him here, because this was the torture. This was both the physical *and* mental torture. If he did not give in, he would die. He could feel his legs weaken with every step. His head was swimming in a fever that had been growing all day, exacerbated by every minute he had remained under the ruthless sun. And the infection in his hands had extended itself up to his elbows. His arms were already dying. The hope that had begun to spark quickly began to wane.

He continued to step, however. Thoughts splashed through his mind with a kaleidoscope of ideas. They could take care of him. They *would* take care of him! All he had to do was turn around, and the human clungen would whisk him off to safety, thinking they had the key to Hun Kanny. They would tend to his wrists, and to his fever. They would surely give him some water. Water! The thought of it alone made him come to a stop. He looked back at the boulder. The clungen was no longer hiding. He was standing in front of the boulder, waiting. No words were spoken; the clungen seemed to know what Luke was thinking. He beckoned Luke toward him with a gentle motion of his hands. It was a gesture of kindness, inveigling Luke back down the mountain. Here, too, was a man; he was not a fiend who felt no sympathy. Luke could see it in his every movement. There was a connection. Luntha had not yet gone through the final transformation that would sever him from the rest of humanity. And he was waiting to tend to Luke's needs. It was such a short way down. Luke could fall and roll to the bottom in a couple of seconds. His shoulder twitched. He began swallowing, in an attempt to draw some saliva down his parched throat. Nothing came. He desperately wanted to go! The desire burned in his veins, an unquenchable fire. And as the temptation began to possess him, he closed his eyes, praying for the strength to fight. The fire only grew hotter, more intense. It was not the same as the burning he felt in his wrists; this fire originated in the very depths of his being. His pounding heart was about to ignite from the blaze in his soul. Yet, somehow he held fast. He was fighting from a deeper, more remote, part of his soul. In a monumental effort, he clarified the dilemma for his overtaxed will. Down meant slavery, and up meant freedom.

He turned and continued, now expecting the clungen to chase him, but he didn't. The cloaked figure remained standing in front of the same boulder, not moving. Luke could feel the eyes following him. They were watching him, waiting for him to die.

"There must be others," he thought, "others who didn't despair, others who are being given this same choice..." But nature was slowly making the choice for him.

Moving his legs was like moving tree trunks, and the footing was growing less stable. His spinning head made it impossible to navigate a true course. There was a rock just ahead of him, jutting up from the side of the mountain. His next task became negotiating all obstacles between him and it. He decided that when he finished this course he would slip in behind the rock and rest for a bit. It certainly was a beautiful evening, he thought, as he looked up into the grand expanse of space to see the stars already beginning to twinkle in the black sky.

He took one more step, but his dizziness caused him to come crashing to his knees. He forced his weight to his right, so he would fall down on the upslope. If he had fallen left, he would have tumbled to the bottom, to Luntha's feet. As he lay there, he realized what had just happened: he had simply prevented himself from rolling down the mountain, and yet it had taken all the energy he had left. When he tried to rise, he couldn't. His arms, which were now swollen as well, were useless. He had no control below his shoulders. Turning his head, he could see the rock in front of him. Thoughts of squirming like an earthworm entered his mind. He could make it to the rock. It was not too far. He could squirm there and rest, and then... and then... and then, nothing. He had not the energy to make it to the next rock, and the next, and the next.

It was over.

He closed his eyes, and the world spun like a merry-go-round. It spun faster and faster. He couldn't make it stop. The nauseating dizziness eventually caused him to vomit for the second time. As he gagged, his stomach forced what little fluid it contained up to his mouth, burning his esophagus. When he parted his lips only a trickle of bilious liquid emerged. This new sensation in his throat cleared his mind, however. He knew quite well that he would soon pass out, and then it would be over. "Jim," he thought, "you'd better not quit!"

He stared at the rock in front of him, which had seemed to be a safe haven such a short while ago. It was only a few feet away, but he would never get there. No more safe havens existed for him in this life; he could go no further. Once again, he thought of that night so long ago. He remembered talking to his parents, telling them how much he yearned to see them again. He yearned to join them in an eternal banquet, where he could bathe in Love forever. And this forever, a universe away, was now his attainable haven.

As the world spun out of control, faster and faster, like a top that accelerated with each turn, he dreamed with them. His entire body had gone numb by now, but his brain still functioned. It functioned enough for him to say goodbye to Kor, to remember Kor's parting wish for him, his mother's prayer... enough for him to welcome his angel as it came for him. Then, while contemplating this heavenly beauty, the top finally spun itself out. He fainted away, and soon thereafter, left this life and was carried off to be reunited with his parents.

****

THE ORDERS whispered to Luntha were quite simple: Wait for him to give up, or watch him die... then, make certain he's dead. Following his orders, he turned to the boulder, and picked up a long lance he had brought for this purpose. Not until his victim fell did he realize that he would have to use it. Nobody, he thought, would choose death. More than that, nobody would choose willfully to suffer as much as this boy had before dying. It was true that Luntha still had human emotions. He was picked because he *was* still human. This was thought to be the one temptation the victim could not overcome: the lie that it was possible to join the dragons and not lose one's humanity. Yet somehow, this weak, dying boy was able to resist... Yet, orders were orders. And he began to climb the mountain toward Luke's body. This final task was merely academic; the boy was dead.

But he found his job more difficult than he had expected. Raising the lance over his head, he held it there. He looked down at the boy's face, awed by its strength. This weak, dead boy in front of him was stronger than the dragons. But orders *were* orders, and he looked up into the night sky, closed his eyes and thrust the lance into Luke's chest, breaking his ribs, piercing his heart. He then tightened his grip and forced the shaft through until its sharp metal head struck the tough mountainside.

Luntha fell to his knees. Scooping up the dead body, he cradled it in his arms. And looking down at that mutilated thing pressed to his chest, he beheld the most beautiful object he had ever seen.

Then he wept.

PART III

HUN KANNY

Bring back, Yahweh, our people from captivity
like torrents in the Negeb!
Those who sow in tears
sing as they reap.

He went off, went off weeping,
carrying the seed.
He comes back, comes back singing.
bringing in his sheaves.
(Psalm 126:4-6)

Chapter Nine

AN UNEXPECTED REPRIEVE

A BOY and his father stood on the shore of Hummingbird Lake throwing rocks into the water. The man was the Rocking champion of the island. But today was not a practice day. It was a day of reprieve – a day to relax with his nine-year old son.

The son was ecstatic. It was the first time he had been outside in seven days. "Hey Dad, do you think it's over? Did we win?" he asked his father.

Smiling at the innocent world of a nine-year old, the father answered, "No, Peter, it's not over. They have the mainland. But for now, we're safe on the island."

"Hey, when do you think they'll start the games again?"

"I don't know. I don't imagine until after the war."

"Think we'll win, Dad?"

"Well, it looks pretty bad at the moment. But yes, I think we'll win." The father threw a rock at a stick in the water forty yards away, attempting to change the topic. All week the people had looked to him to lead the defense of the island, and now he was blessed with this unexpected rest.

Sometime, in the dark hours of the morning, the dragon left. Abruptly and inexplicably, it turned and flew away. He knew that if he didn't take this opportunity to relax with his son, he would be overwhelmed with grief. He felt completely unprepared, insufficient to be the leader of the island. Yet, this was the position providence had forced upon him, so he would not allow himself to be overwhelmed with grief, or joy, or any other emotion. Right now, Peter's father wanted nothing more than to get their minds off the war altogether, if only for a few short hours. He hit the stick, and the attempt was successful.

"Nice shot, Dad! Bobby Hawkey said he's gonna beat you this year... Ain't no chance is there Dad?"

"There's always a chance, son. But I think Mr. Hawkey may have to wait until next year." He winked at Peter. "I'm still at the top of my game."

Peter began throwing rocks at targets in the water. Then after missing his first ten shots, he started skipping stones. The shore on which they stood had little incline. It seemed to creep out of the water, and was covered with smooth stones. Behind them was the upslope. Hummingbird Lake was some six hundred acres, surrounded by tall hills, which blocked any wind, except on the truly blustery days. Although there was a waterfall at the other end, it was too far away to disturb the placid surface of the lake in front of them. Thus, it was ideal for skipping.

"Hey Dad, wouldn't it be awesome if you were the Rocking champion and I was the skipping champion?"

"Yeah, Pete, that would be awesome." Peter's father tried to sound excited, but skipping had always played second fiddle to Rocking. It was fun, to be sure, with all its different categories: number of skips, distance from the first skip to the last, and so on. But everyone on the island knew that skipping was the undercard. The main event was Rocking. It always had been, and, if they survived the war, it always would be. The inhabitants of the island were the best rock throwers in Calapanta. So the champion was *the* best – period.

The father continued picking off target after target. There were no multiple categories in Rocking, no gimmicks, no frills. It was a combination of strength and accuracy, and Peter's father had not been beaten in three years.

"Hey, Dad," Peter asked, "you wanna skip rocks with me?"

Now came the moment of truth. Was he enjoying his son or perfecting his skill? The man dropped his throwing rock, slowly bent down, and picked up a smooth, flat stone. "Alright, Pete, what do you want to play?"

"I don't know. Whatever you like best. Hey, I'm pretty good at all of them."

The man chuckled at the boy's confidence. He loved to be with his son, and was happy to have this chance to play. It was a blessing after that first week of battle, and he wasn't sure how long the break would last.

"Hey, Pete, hey." He ruffled Peter's hair and laughed. "I just had a new idea for a game."

"What's that?" Peter asked. His father could tell that he was interested.

"It's called synchronized skipping. We throw the stones at the same time, and try to see if we can get them to skip next to each other."

"Hey, sounds like fun!"

But after their first few throws, Peter began to lose interest. None were synchronized, and the war began to consume his attention again. "Hey, Tommy told me that he saw a dragon."

"Tommy Tripp is a funny kid. Sometimes I think he's mistaken in what he sees though." This was as soft as he could put it. He didn't want to insult the boy, and Peter knew that when his father called one of his friends funny, it meant that he liked him. "What was he doing outside anyway?" he asked.

"He said that a couple days ago one of the wooden boards fell down..."

"Sounds like it fell on his head," his father interrupted.

"So you really don't believe him?" Peter was disappointed.

"You're going to hear a lot of crazy things as the war goes on. The last thing we need is for Tommy Tripp to get all you guys worked up over what he claims he saw. Yes, there *are* dragons out there, but remember this: Never stand in awe of them. Never!" He caught himself before he became too serious. That was the last thing he wanted today. Changing his tone he said, "... it weakens the knees." He gave a slight snicker, "Tommy Tripp – seein' the world!" Then he opened his eyes wide with excitement, "Why don't we get back to our game? I think I figured out what we're doin' wrong."

He tweaked their timing a touch, and their next throw was vastly improved.

"Hey, Dad, that was awesome!" Peter exclaimed.

"It was good, but we can do better. Here let's give it another go." He picked up two identical skipping rocks. "Use this one, Pete. I bet it's darn near perfect this time."

Their form was identical; both released at the same time, and as the stones were about to land on their second skip, something bobbed up out of the water between them. They missed it by inches. The stones continued on their way as the object disappeared below the surface.

Chapter Ten

LONG LOST FRIENDS

JIM BROKE through the surface of the lake and drank in the fresh air. His vision was blurred from water and adrenaline. A spray of darkened colors slowly congealed into shoreline, trees, and hills. He could see that he was treading water in the middle of a lake on a clear night. The moon was the brightest he'd ever seen. This must be far from the city, he reasoned, for the sky was undisturbed by any artificial light.

He swam to the shore, slipped onto the smooth stones and rested. Gazing up into the night he tried to reason through everything that had just happened to him. It made no sense. Awakening from a crazy dream, he seemed to enter an even crazier one. While he was still pondering this, the dim stars directly above him were blotted out. Something enormous was flying just over the treetops. And he wondered if the demented dream would ever end. He began wondering if he were the one who had gone mad. These visions could all be the phantasms of a deranged mind.

After the silhouette disappeared beyond the western hills, he sat up and looked around. The feeling that he had seen this place before slowly crept over him. It was an unsettling thought. And it became even more disturbing when he realized that he had indeed seen it before, but only in his mind's eye. If this were the place he thought it was, then there would be a waterfall at the far end of the lake. He had to dare himself to listen. And when he did, he was tempted to doubt his own ears as they heard the rush of the water in the distance. He was off, swimming across the lake – at an unsustainable pace to start, and then he slowed to something a bit more reasonable. He was a good swimmer, but not great. Every so often, he needed to stop and tread water as he caught his breath. Then he would continue his swim. Somewhere along the way, the cloth bandage slipped off his foot, but he didn't notice. He had his mind set on a single purpose – making it to the falls. However, as he approached his destination, he swam to the shore to sit and reflect upon what he was about to do.

Excitement began to grip him. It was an intense, nervous feeling, but it was refreshing. His adrenaline began pumping again, and he rose to his feet. Kor was right! It suddenly seemed foolish to have ever doubted him.

While standing there, a stone's throw from the waterfall, he observed the dark outlines of strange trees in the distance. They graced the hills surrounding the lake, their palms spread out like large, exotic fans welcoming him to the island. They were traveler's trees, but he had never seen them before. He had never even imagined them before. If it were not for the moon's unusual brightness, he wouldn't have noticed them now, yet they were peaceful and inviting, and they gave him the strength to open his mind to the full reality of which Kor had told him the previous morning. He tried to let go of his own little world, which he had been holding onto so terribly hard. This place did not exist because he had imagined it. He had imagined it because it existed. And he had been given an incomplete vision. Those traveler's trees were real. He knew they were. They completed the scenery, and they were just as real as the waterfall and the cave behind the waterfall. He decided that he could only be insane if there were, in fact, no cave. Such were his thoughts before he continued on. And the excitement grew as he approached the falls. He didn't want to go around behind them to check for the cave. Somehow, that was not appropriate. When about to discover one's own sanity, it must be done with conviction. He waded into the lake, and walked through the falling water, closing his eyes. Then he let himself fall forward. If he were loony, he told himself, he would break his nose on the rocks.

He landed on the soft, sandy floor of the cave's mouth and rolled around in elated oblivion. He forgot all his troubles, all his worries, just rolling in the sand. To hold your own sanity in doubt, to seriously question the stability of your own mind, and then to break through – this can be the most thrilling adventure of them all! And Jim had a right to a few moments of oblivion.

The adventure was not over, however. He collected himself, and began to rethink the situation: Stackingsdale had been emptied; he did not know where his family was; and, if everything Kor said was true, he was needed to fight dragons. Sure, Hun Kanny had always won in his stories, but this was reality, and reality was daunting. It sobered him.

He resolved not to be intimidated by the frightening possibilities of the future as long as there was something to be done in the present. The search must begin. The cave lay before him, and Hun Kanny lay sleeping somewhere within.

Anyone who has gone spelunking knows the darkness Jim entered after he took the first turn. He remembered reading a short story in class his freshman year about the men who had explored the deepest cave ever discovered. The story did not help ease his anxiety. Those men had lights and yet still battled with the cave's unknown dangers. He was being guided by his hands and by his memory. And in his memory the cave was not this dark. He remembered it being dimly lit as Hun Kanny emerged from it. But this was not pretend. This was a cave, a deep, winding cave, and after many turns, he yearned to go back to the opening, to light. He could no longer go back however, for he no longer knew the way. To add to his misery his heel was throbbing again. He tried to ignore the pain, focusing on continuing down. And so he did.

Jim soon realized that he would not be able to maintain his composure if he focused on his situation: He was in a place the sun's rays could not touch – pure darkness all the time; he was lost; at times the walls closed in so closely that he was forced to squirm his way between the damp stone. This was obviously not the way Hun Kanny could take to emerge from his cave. Jim felt the panic; it rose from the pit of his gut, and attempted to consume him. But before the uncontrollable shaking began, he managed to force it down by focusing on his specific task at hand. He must continue down. When put this way it became quite simple.

He began to walk with his eyes closed. It was much less disconcerting than seeing nothing with them open. It felt like a game of blind man's bluff, and he was slightly more at ease. With eyes shut tight, he sat down, ripped another piece of cloth off his t-shirt and tied it around his heel. He stood up, ready to play the game; Hun Kanny was the opponent. When found, Hun Kanny would laugh. He would laugh a loud, gleeful laugh. Jim knew that it would be grand to hear him laugh like that. He had not laughed in any of the stories and Jim wondered why. Why hadn't he written one sentence about Hun Kanny's laughter? And he felt sorry about this. No one had ever experienced Hun Kanny's laugh. They had experienced him killing the enemy – killing enemy after enemy. Here, once again, Hun Kanny was needed to kill. But he was good. And he must have a good laugh. It was sure to be a booming, raucous, infectious guffaw. Jim started to chuckle just thinking about it, and he was surprised at the noise he created. He hooted. It felt good to hoot.

"Hey!" he shouted. "Hey, hey, hey!" The silence was broken. The haunting halls of the cave seemed far less menacing without the consuming silence. So he commenced singing. If it were not for the unsteady path beneath his feet, one of which was cushioned with a cloth strap, he would have started skipping. He even laughed at the way this would kill the mood of a "deep, dark cave". He sang song after song, entire songs, pieces of songs, making up words to songs. He even grunted out songs as he forced his way through the tight spots, trusting that the hall would open wide once more. Then, while nearing the end of his repertoire, he heard an echo. It was deep and hollow. He continued to sing, but more slowly now. His voice then lowered until the song became no more than a whisper; finally, in the middle of the refrain, it disappeared altogether. He knew where he was.

He hooted again, but this time, for a different reason. The acoustics were unmistakable He was in a large open room, and when he took one more step, he was not surprised to feel his foot enter the water. Yes, this was it. He was serious now; the songs and games were over.

He called out Hun Kanny's name. He did not know what he would do once Hun Kanny answered, but he kept calling, hearing his echo. It was when Hun Kanny failed to answer that he became frightened. He called loudly, yelling, screaming Hun Kanny's name. He was calling for an old, lost friend – pleading to him for forgiveness. Then his voice began cracking. He was crying now, weeping spasmodically through his screams. How could he have forgotten about him? He wondered if Hun Kanny would ever answer. Perhaps he had gone into such a deep sleep that he could not be wakened. There was no one else to revive him. Nobody had come down here before. Those on the island had never risked the path, not knowing that Hun Kanny lived here. Jim knew this. Hun Kanny was the only other person down here, and he was not answering.

Jim dove into the water but came up soon. The next time, he took in as much air as he could and slowly exhaled as he descended. He dove deep, much deeper this time, but could still not touch the bottom. He came to the surface and tried to swim back to dry land, but he had lost his sense of direction, and swam much further than he knew he should. Finally, he struck a wall and followed it until it led him to a shore. He could not be certain that this was the same shore from which he had originally jumped, but he crawled up onto it anyway. Defeated, he slumped onto the floor of the cave. There was nothing else to do, so, physically and emotionally spent, he decided to rest. Soon, due to utter exhaustion, he was fast asleep.

****

HE WAS jerked awake. By what, he did not know, nor did he know how long he had slept. He began to appreciate the invention of the watch. It was indeed frustrating to awaken from his slumber into a stillness where there are no clues as to what time it is. He was very much afraid that this could be the summation of the rest of his life: a timeless void, trapped in darkness.

Then he realized what had awakened him. Pangs of guilt pressed down upon him. He had not paid them much attention through the chaos, but now that he was rested and still, he could feel their sharp pricks. He remembered Kor. The conversation was anything but ambiguous. But, in a regrettable act of mistrust, Jim had refused. And now his hometown was empty, and his family could all be dead.

No. Giving up was not an option.

He must jump back into the water, and this time, he must find something. He comforted himself with the thought that there were many worse ways to die than by drowning. At the moment, however, he could not think of any. It seems to be the case, that the worst way to die is the one that's being faced. And so it took a supreme act of courage for him to dive back into the water. He prayed as he swam through the darkness until he hit the wall. The time had come to go under. He had heard somewhere that if he faked hyperventilating before taking a deep breath he'd be able to hold his breath longer. Having no better idea and disappointed by his previous attempt, he decided to give it a try. He panted in short gasps until he felt light-headed. He stopped, inhaled deeply, filling his lungs, and his faintness disappeared.

Then he dove headfirst and kicked his way down. After only a few feet, he located an opening in the wall, and, without thinking, entered it. He swam across the bottom of the tunnel feeling if it were leading up or down. It continued to lead down. After only a minute, his lungs started to burn. He could feel them straining for oxygen. But he continued down. Then, when he had almost gasped for air unconsciously, he thought about turning back, but it was too late for that. He would never make it back to the surface in the cave. The tunnel needed to open, or he would drown. It continued to lead down. He was fighting his lungs now. They had a mind of their own, and this mind could not understand why he had taken so long for his next breath. It would force him to breathe. His swimming stalled, and his hands began to shake, then his arms. Then his whole body shook in violent convulsions. His heart rate jumped, as the pulsating organ frantically pumped blood to the oxygen starved muscles. He could feel it pounding in his chest; he could hear it in his ears. Consciousness began to fade, but he could not allow his lungs to win the battle. He could not breathe... he must not breathe. His brain was trying to make sense of the situation. It sent impulses to his eyes, and he saw various colors for the first time since he entered the cave. He saw spots racing haphazardly through the bright reds and deep blues that filled his vision. And his lungs tightened, stronger and stronger. His trachea was working in tandem with his lungs, pressing his throat, trying to force it open. His tongue remained affixed to the roof of his mouth preventing the air from escaping. And he kept his lips shut like a vice.

He could no longer swim. The trembling had ceased; now his muscles were tightening into a large cramp. It started in his gut and worked its way down his legs, then up through his arms. Blood rushed to his head; the pressure was unbearable. He felt as though it would pop, explode, bloodying the deep waters of the cave. Meanwhile, the optic vessels, on the verge of erupting, had forced his eyes to roll back into his head.

Then, as he was losing consciousness, he heard someone shout, "I'm holding on for you!" The words were crisp, as if the person were right next to him. He couldn't know who was speaking, but he listened.

As he held on, delaying what appeared to be inevitable, something grabbed him. It wrapped an arm around his torso and placed a hand over his face, closing his nose and mouth. Then it rushed him back up the tunnel. Accelerating faster than a sailfish, it reached the surface within seconds. Jim gasped for life, filling his lungs with the damp subterranean air. It was the most refreshing breath he had ever breathed.

Then he began panting for air, and as he rapidly inhaled he felt no further relief. Forcing himself to slow his respiration, he sucked in deeply and held the air down. His lungs burned again, but this time with life giving oxygen.

They felt as though they would burst, being stretched to full capacity. Then he exhaled, and repeated the process. The uncontrollable spasms in his arms and legs resumed. And spots once again raced randomly in the darkness. But he was not bothered by these discomforts. It was his need for air that consumed him. He didn't even notice that he had been carried to the shore and placed on solid ground. When he finally did recover, he realized that he was being hugged by something large.

"Hun Kanny," he said. The thing hugged him tighter, and he knew it was his "old, lost friend".

He had entered his own tomb to discover vitality. It was not until he was called upon to face death that he had truly lived. And the incredible had happened. It was not some cheap trick like so many daredevils who seem to hold their life of little worth. No, he did not wish to die, and yet he risked dying to save others. That is a strength that resides in no human. And yet every human is capable of it if he is open to it.

The incredible *had* happened! Hun Kanny had awoken and was holding Jim in an embrace of pure friendship and joy. The time had come to make things right. Jim knew it was impossible for him to do it alone. He had needed to find Hun Kanny.

He pulled on the schwah. Hun Kanny responded immediately. Knowing what Jim was thinking, he picked him up into his arms. Jim took another deep breath and was plunged back under. This time he was breathless from the sheer speed. They were through the tunnel and ascending to the surface of Hummingbird Lake before Jim thought about exhaling. They slowed down, and their heads broke through together to see two stones sailing toward them. Quickly, Hun Kanny dipped back under the water.

When they reemerged they could see a man running into the water toward them as he yelled something incoherent to a boy on the shore.

Chapter Eleven

MIXED EMOTIONS

"IT'S HIM!" the man yelled. "It's him!" He splashed into the water to meet them. The boy stood on the shore, confused. The man looked back, and spurted out muddled directions to his son.

Hun Kanny carried Jim over to the man who had waded fifteen feet into the lake. The man continued yelling. "You've come! They said you were dead, but I never believed it!" Hun Kanny stopped in front of him.

"It's me, Samuel, Samuel Biggs," he said, fearing he had been forgotten. But when the schwah smiled at him, he knew he was remembered.

Peter rushed in, finally understanding what was going on. This was Hun Kanny! This was the schwah his father had told him so many stories about! Though he was already five when Hun Kanny fell into his deep sleep, he was but two the last time he had seen him. Thus he had become a legend for the boy... the hero of a myth from the past. But the myth had just come true.

He was giddy with excitement and danced a silly dance through the water. When he finally made it to Hun

Kanny, he hugged him. Samuel looked at his son again. Yes, he loved the confidence. Deep inside, he wished that he had given the schwah a spontaneous hug. It was then that he noticed Jim for the first time.

Jim had never been comfortable meeting new people. So, impolite or not, he stared. He stared at Samuel through his bloodshot eyes.

"Goodness! What happened to you, son?" asked Samuel.

"Me, um... I almost drowned," he managed. Hun Kanny carried him to the shore and laid him down. Jim was able to look upon the schwah for the first time. He felt as though he had seen him before, and then again, as though he had not – as if his imagination had detracted from Hun Kanny's appearance, darkened it, made it more mundane, something he would see in a book. The reality, however, was inimitable, even in one's imagination. The great schwah prince was truly awesome to behold.

He stood nearly fifteen feet tall and shimmered gold. The golden hue slowly darkened into a deep charcoal down his thick, long tail. And his trunk-like legs, golden and muscular, were the image of stability, carrying his massive body. The gold again changed its hue as it ran down his powerful arms, gradually dissolving into vermilion red hands. A thick neck supported his intimidating head, yet there was peace in his expression; his strong countenance was gentle though hewn from rock. He was indescribably handsome, majestic, and his wings were priceless jewels all over. They spread out a dazzling canopy, revealing layer upon layer of shimmering colors, iridescent in the sunlight – bright yellow to soft green to light blue.

Hun Kanny covered Jim with those brilliant wings, inspecting his foot. The second bandage had slipped off somewhere in the water, revealing an infection spreading from the gash in his heel. The schwah began to massage the foot, rubbing the heel as Jim tightly clenched his teeth. He rubbed deeper and deeper, and it was all Jim could do not to cry out in pain. Then Hun Kanny let go, folded his magnificent wings behind his back, and reached down to help Jim stand. When Jim was back on his feet, his wound was gone. Hun Kanny was not only a killer, he discovered, he was also a healer.

"Wow!" was all he could say.

"Wow's right!" said Samuel, "We could've used that this past week!" Then, realizing that in the excitement he had failed to greet the boy, he introduced himself, "Like I said, my name's Samuel." Then he turned to his son, "This is Peter. We were just out here to rest from the war. It would've been a shame if you survived the past week and then drowned in the lake."

"I wasn't here last week," said Jim, "I've never been here before."

A light went on in Samuel's mind. His face brightened, and he raised his hands in excited gesticulations. "Hun Kanny!... The legend!... The legend is true!" He was stammering like a giddy schoolboy. Apparently, something Jim had said had caused Samuel to grow quite animated. And it was with this childlike enthusiasm that he pleaded with the two newcomers: "Can you both come with me to the village?"

"Sure," answered Jim, speaking for Hun Kanny. The schwah didn't appear to mind; he was content simply being with Jim. And there was a unique, almost maternal, characteristic in the way he gazed down at his boy.

Looking up at Hun Kanny, Jim had the sensation of being back in a dream world again. His mind was having difficulty making sense of what was happening. Before following Samuel and Peter up the hill, he lifted his foot to inspect it one more time. At least the injury had been a constant reminder of reality, but now he could only stare in wonder at the unblemished skin covering his heel. Not wanting to be a cause for delay, he quickly put his foot back down and walked up the hill.

"Are you from Maine?" asked Samuel as Jim caught up to him.

"Yes," replied Jim. He knew he should have been surprised by the question, shocked even. But he was growing accustomed to the uncanny way people seemed to know things about him. If Samuel *didn't* know he was from Maine, now *that* would have been truly bizarre.

Samuel raised his eyebrows and gave a soft whistle. "Out of Hummingbird Lake, too... that lake," he thumbed back at the water, "Just like the legend foretold." He looked at Jim. "We had almost given up on you – 'a boy from the land of Maine'. I started thinking you were just fiction, that there would be no one to wake up Hun Kanny." He slapped Jim roughly on the back. "But, you've come, my boy, you've finally come!"

It was late in the afternoon by the time they arrived at the village. Jim could see it through the trees. The bamboo huts with their thatched roofs caused him to wonder if this place were primitive or just merely "tropical". Eventually he would learn that comparing them to the paradigm of his own civilization was an erroneous exercise anyway. Approaching the village, which looked quite similar to the one Hun Kanny had saved several times in his grade school stories, he didn't know what to think. As they walked through the last row of palm trees and actually entered the village, thinking was no longer possible. Spotted by some of the islanders, an instantaneous celebration began. It was a whirlwind of cheering and dancing. Jim was held up as a hero. They carried him over their heads. They heaped flowers upon Hun Kanny, rejoicing that salvation had finally come.

Jim didn't like it. The praise and adulation sickened him. He didn't know anything about the battles, but he knew that it was all far from over. His family was still missing, and "salvation" for this village wouldn't bring them back. He apologized profusely, asking to be put down and telling them that he was tired and needed sleep. It took a while for the villagers to hear him, but once they did they decided to bring him to Samuel's hut where he could rest. Jim knew by their manner that they were disappointed, but he didn't care. When asked if there was anything he needed, anything they could do, he shook his head, and then, not so politely, shut the door.

The celebration outside eventually subsided. Samuel seized the opportunity to take Hun Kanny to the injured in the makeshift infirmary. It was a simple, large section behind the huts, roped off from the rest of the village. There were rows of cots filled with islanders wounded in battle. Thin blankets attached to bamboo provided shade. As Hun Kanny made his way there the people followed. They wanted to see what the schwah prince would do. They didn't want to let him out of their sight; he seemed too good to be true, and it was all Samuel could do to make them wait outside the ropes and watch while he went in.

Many of the wounded were still unconscious, and others had been drugged with natural painkillers. But those who were conscious and aware sat up to see the large "creature" coming toward them. They were frightened but trusting, for walking next to it was Samuel. It didn't take long for them to realize who this creature was, and, once they saw him healing the wounded, there was no more room for fear. Rather, there was a joyous anticipation as each waited impatiently for Hun Kanny to come to his cot. Soon things were under control, and Samuel asked one of the villagers to assist the schwah in anything he might need. Then Samuel left to go check on Jim.

When he entered his hut, he could see that Jim was not sleeping, but he didn't say anything. Jim was the first to speak. "I'll be honest. I have no idea what's going on. What *I* need is for Hun Kanny to find *my* family. I woke up last night, and they were gone; the city I live in... the entire city was empty, and all I know is that it has something to do with this war." Samuel remained silent. He stared out the open doorway, thinking. He hadn't considered the situation from Jim's point of view before, what it would take to bring a boy here from "the land of Maine" and away from his family. The boy must be terribly confused, and he didn't know how to comfort him.

"What kind of war is this?" Jim asked, breaking the silence again.

Samuel continued looking out the doorway for a few more seconds, wondering if it was prudent to answer the question. Then, deciding that whether Jim liked it or not, he *was* the boy who had wakened Hun Kanny... and he *was* from Maine, Samuel turned to face him. Keeping Jim from the truth would serve no purpose. "We're at war with the dragons," Samuel answered, "and we're losing. This island is the only place in our country they haven't conquered. The mainland's controlled by them; the entire continent could be for all we know, and last night we were on the verge of falling to one of them... but it flew away."

"Dragons? How many dragons?" Jim demanded.

"Three. But we've only seen one of the black ones. They're as black as soot. No one's seen the red one yet. Our hope is that it's still in exile, but I doubt it."

"It left last night?" asked Jim. "When?"

"We don't know exactly," said Samuel.

"Can you guess?" Jim pleaded, "Two? Three? Four?"

"I'd say some time before four."

Jim turned away from Samuel. "I'm no hero," he mumbled.

****

HUN KANNY continued healing the wounded. He knew that a great battle was coming, and he needed the villagers healthy and ready to fight. Samuel knew this as well, but he remained with Jim. There was nothing he could do to help Hun Kanny at the moment. It was the boy who needed Samuel's attention, for it was the boy who was lonely and confused about his situation. Jim would be able to understand much better if he knew the history of this war. To truly comprehend its history, to fully grasp its significance, he would have to be told the legend of which he was a part. So Samuel went back to the beginning.... to the Legend of Hummingbird Lake:

THE LAKE was a haven for hummingbirds long, long ago – the various little "flying jewels" used to hover over the flowers, amongst the flowers, in the flowers. And they were protected by their schwah prince. Different types of schwahs are attached to different creatures: some to tigers, some to crocodiles, and so on. The princes, the most powerful of the schwahs, are attached to the smallest of birds, the hummingbirds. And when Hummingbird Lake was first created, a great schwah prince was put in charge over it. But now the lake was empty of them, their iridescent display utterly destroyed by a hellish decision the schwah prince, the very one who was supposed to protect them, had made centuries ago.

The mighty prince had been the ruler of the island as well, but it was in his beautiful lake that he took his greatest pride. He would stroll along its shores beckoning to the birds. They would flitter to him as soon as he called, and the smell of sweet nectar would tickle his nose. He loved to have them dart around his head, and would laugh a joyful laugh, content on his island, his paradise... Then one day he discovered something he could not accept. Humans were coming. He despised humans, for he knew what they would do to his island. They would exploit his paradise. And it became worse. He learned that he was to keep this lake beautiful for them, for their enjoyment. "Never!" he thought – never could he be subservient to humans. They were beneath him – weak, disgusting creatures who couldn't possibly appreciate the beauty he had created. It was more than he could endure. And so he chose to reject the duty he had been given. It was this choice that corrupted his nature, transforming him into a dragon.

Knowing he could not prevent humans from inhabiting the island, for they were already coming, he chose the power to kill, to destroy the beauty of the lake entirely. A few hummingbirds managed to escape, not to return until the dragon was no more. Most of them, however, innocently drank from the flowers their former prince placed around the lake. The nectar from these flowers was poison. Soon the lake's surface was coated with myriad hummingbird corpses. Their perfect little bodies lay floating for days. Any of the new inhabitants, the humans, attempting to approach the waters were scorched to death by its former guardian, and the trespassers' bodies were thrown in to join the hummingbirds'.

Eventually, maggots filled the birds' flesh, and the lake became rancid from the floating rot. Finally, the evil schwah swam into the rank water, feasting on the decomposing corpses, signifying the completion of his demonic transformation. And he grew. He grew two, three times his original size, glutting himself with filth, learning to hate all he once loved. When he had engorged himself with the last putrefied body the metamorphosis was over. It was finished; this once beautiful prince was now the blood red dragon.

Before it could ravage the entire island, another schwah prince was sent to duel with it. This other schwah was Hun Kanny, Calapanta's new protector. He was much smaller than the dragon, but he was strong and quick. And he was brave. Dragons are despicable – evil, malicious, even powerful, but not brave. And their cowardice is equaled only by their pride. The dragon taunted its puny foe, reviling him with supreme disdain. No one who willingly served humans, it thought, could match it in battle. This new contemptuous thing would be destroyed, and then the dragon would enslave the Calapantans. They would be subservient to it. The thought of being subservient to them was simply laughable.

The dragon was greatly mistaken.

When the two fought, what the dragon thought would be an easy victory turned into a desperate struggle. And as the flames rose high into the blackened sky, Hun Kanny struck for the heart. He was on the dragon in a flash, pounding its chest, and the dragon's size was of no use to it. In fact, Hun Kanny used it to his advantage. It was too large, its arms too fat to clutch at anything close. Thus the schwah prince was able to cling tightly, breathing his fiery breath into the dragon's breast. The two fell, intertwined, from the smoke into the steaming lake. The water could not quench the flames, and the Red Dragon felt the fire burning into its scales. They then rolled onto the shore of Hummingbird Lake, and the beast squealed in pain, offering to share its power if Hun Kanny would let it go, tempting him with promises of unfathomable glory. The schwah prince would not give in. He knew that when dealing with a dragon, one must never listen to it. No, he would have the dragon's heart. He must if he were to slay the beast. Then, once its heart was removed, the ground beneath the Red Dragon's heartless body would open, and it would be swallowed into the bowels of the very earth it had originally been meant to protect.

But before Hun Kanny ripped through its powerful chest, the dragon spit fire into the distance, and he could do nothing to stop it. As the flames spewed forth from its mouth, the island was slowly being ignited. Calapanta's worthy guardian knew that if he were to save his country, he must let the dragon go. For if he held on until its death the islanders would be burned alive. This was not an option. Thus the Red Dragon survived, fleeing far from Calapanta. Hun Kanny had forced it into exile, but he could not destroy it. The vegetative beauty of Hummingbird Lake was revived, but the birds themselves remained absent. There was nothing he could do to bring them back.

As long as Hun Kanny remained vigilant the Red Dragon would not return either. And he *did* remain vigilant. Legends grew through the centuries of battles, epic battles from days of yore, in defense of the peoples of Calapanta. The great schwah prince held fast to his duty and protected his people against marauding invaders from other lands, against turmoil from within, and against freakish monsters too abominable to believe.

Then came peace. The people wanted to deify him, but he firmly rejected it. This continued on for some years, and eventually he went into hiding. Slowly, as peace continued to reign, the praise changed into unbelief. Centuries had passed since the Red Dragon had been banished from Calapanta, and a generation grew up that had experienced nothing but peace; they had no reason to doubt its stability. And the thought that the peace was somehow connected to this creature became something for the children or the superstitious to believe. Dragons and other such evil creations were myths, they had thought, pure myths... fantasies for simpletons.

Those on the mainland had been the first to lose faith in Hun Kanny as a guardian of Calapanta. They began to treat him as some exotic animal, a unique creature to show to their children. If he were truly intelligent, they reasoned, he would be able to speak or to write. But he behaved like so many other animals, hiding from humans. These people set up little expeditions, waiting in the mountains where he liked to roam, and then they would stare. Soon, staring was not enough, and as he visited the mainland less and less, many began to view him as something to conquer. Groups of Calapantans, the very people he had fought so diligently to protect, attempted to track him down to kill him. He had become nothing more than a potential trophy to them. These hunting parties were never endorsed by the rulers of the country, but they turned a blind eye to them. He was technically a "protected animal", but they couldn't see any practical use for him. It was of greater importance, they thought, to focus on the more pragmatic laws. And so Hun Kanny slowly vanished from them.

On the island, however, he was treated with a certain respect. But it was the respect one would give a gentle tiger, or a peaceful grizzly bear. And as for intelligence, he was no more than a dolphin or a monkey in their eyes. Eventually, it became so rare to actually see him that many became convinced the schwah himself was a myth. But a few *did* remain who knew how to communicate with him, who knew he was the true protector of Calapanta. And these select few – the "simpletons" as viewed by the rest of the Calapantans – understood the schwah. They knew the secret of silence... and they knew his sorrow.

Samuel was one of these precious few. He saw his fellow countrymen belittling this wonderful creature but could do nothing to stop them. And when the inevitable finally happened, he was in no way surprised. Hun Kanny simply disappeared. He went into his deep sleep, leaving the country unprotected.

Samuel knew the rest of the legend as well, but he didn't know how to distinguish fact from fiction. It was not until Hun Kanny had left that he began to believe more and more of the legend as fact. While most people soon doubted a creature called Hun Kanny had ever roamed their countryside, while those who had never seen him mocked those who professed his existence, Samuel's belief was strengthening. However, he was never sure about the boy from Maine, the one linked to Hun Kanny. Samuel became more convinced each day that this boy was the result of a storyteller's overactive imagination. According to legend, the schwah prince had been intrinsically connected to this boy since the beginning. During the centuries preceding the boy's birth, Hun Kanny waited with excited anticipation for his coming. This kept him vigilant. But once the boy, who had loved him so tenderly as a child, began to forget about him, viewing him as impractical and childish, he slipped into his deep forgetful sleep.

Then came the rumors. Dragons were conquering far off lands. The mainland laughed. The islanders were incredulous. But when the refugees began to trickle in, they were difficult to ignore. These few who had managed to flee the dragons' captivity came with incredible, horrific stories of fire, death, and destruction, and many Calapantans were forced to believe. They looked through the old books, the legends, searching for means to bring back their guardian. They could find nothing to waken him from his deep sleep – nothing save this "fictional" boy.

The island then looked to Samuel to organize their defense. He was the only one who seemed to know what to do. He told no one that he did not believe in the boy from Maine. Rather, he impressed upon them his firm belief that Hun Kanny would indeed return to defend Calapanta. Thus the laughing stock who naively believed in children's stories had become their leader. And he began praying for the strength to lead them.

The dragons swept through the mainland in a week, but could not conquer the fighting spirit of the islanders. One of the reasons for this was Samuel's foresight. Of course, in his humility, he would never admit this. He said that it was because the dragons had sent mere clungens to do battle. And these clungens had been unprepared for a real fight. The mainland had offered them no opposition – its weapons impotent to provide the slightest defense. But when they arrived at the island's shores they reeled back from the force of the islanders' weapons. This was Hun Kanny's island, his fortress; anything on it could be used to fight the dragons or their clungens.

Here the history was interrupted, and Samuel had to explain to Jim what a clungen was and why weapons would have no effect on them. Once Jim understood, he asked why the Red Dragon had sent clungens instead of coming itself. The island, he thought, would have been the first place in Calapanta it would have tried to conquer. Samuel couldn't answer this question with certainty. The islanders had discussed it, and no one knew the reason. His personal feeling was that the island was the place of the Red Dragon's defeat, and it was in no way anxious to come back here. Then again, it could be that the fear of Hun Kanny was keeping it away. They didn't know how much the Red Dragon knew. It might not be convinced that the protector of Calapanta was in a deep enough sleep to surrender his island without a fight. And it was only a small island. If Hun Kanny were not defending it, then the clungens should be able to defeat it with ease, and if he were, then the dragons would plan their attack accordingly. However, the unexpected occurred. Hun Kanny did not defend the islanders, but the clungens could not defeat them. The dragons soon realized that the island would not be taken unless they went in and conquered it themselves. Thus, yesterday, about midday, a black dragon appeared on the horizon. The islanders' fears were realized and it was difficult for Samuel to prevent them from losing hope. By nightfall, it had destroyed most of their defenses; they were about to fall.

****

"**THEN, WELL,** ...you know what happened; it left, and here you are," Samuel concluded.

Jim did not know how to respond to this. It was too much. He was not a hero. He knew that. He did not belong in legends. His instinct was to deny it all, but before he could speak, one of the islanders entered the hut.

"We've finished digging," the newcomer announced. "Are you ready?"

"Yes, I'll be right there," answered Samuel, and the islander left.

Jim noticed that the messenger had seemed somber, almost mournful. "What's going on?" he asked.

"Your coming today was providential. It gave us something to celebrate amidst the sorrow. You see, there are many dead to bury. And I've asked each person to dig a grave. They won't be dumped into a mass one... I dug mine this morning."

"But they seemed so happy when we got here," said Jim.

"Elation I would call it. They were elated to see the two of you. Interestingly enough, they wouldn't have been as ecstatic if they weren't feeling so..." Samuel searched for the right word, "...disconsolate. Joy and sorrow – it's an interesting mix, but life's full of it, you know. Sometimes it seems they go hand in hand." Samuel rose to his feet. He spoke without emotion, and Jim was amazed at his apparent apathy. He didn't realize how deeply Samuel felt the pain of yesterday's battle. He needed to speak this way; it was the

only way he could stay strong, for the village and for himself.
"After the burial," he said, "we'll start preparing for tomorrow.
The dragon is sure to come back soon, but this time," and a
glimmer came to his eye, "we have more hope – thanks to
you."

"Please stop thanking me," begged Jim. He knew that
everything he had done since he had left his house was done
out of compulsion. There was nothing courageous about that.
And the repercussions of his failure yesterday morning
continued to plague him. "If I was truly a hero, you wouldn't
have lost half your people, and my family would still be at
home, as if... as if nothing had happened." He stood to follow
Samuel.

Samuel turned to face him once more. "You can come
if you want, but I'm not encouraging you to." Samuel
appeared to be ignoring what Jim had said. "Each has his own
grave, but there are no caskets," he warned. "And it was a
terrible battle."

Jim hesitated. Then he followed. His life had been
spared several times in the last few hours, and he had done
nothing to deserve it. He could easily have been another dead
body, with no one to mourn him. Yes, he would join them to
bury their dead, the dead whom he could have saved if he had
acted in time. The least he could do now was to pray for them.

He looked out to see the dark hues that follow a
glorious sunset. Hun Kanny came to join him as he stared into
the twilight. The celebrations of the evening had transformed
into a nighttime cortege. The people were making their way
up a nearby hill in the solemn procession. It was truly
beautiful, he thought. There was something ethereal about the

scene: the mourners slowly walking past him under the clear night sky, disappearing into the palm trees over the hill, in silence, and the stars increasing in intensity as the glow from the sun's rays softly descended beyond the western mountains.

This sense of beauty slowly waned as he made his way up the hill. He could see the flickering of the torches in the distance. They had been set up around the gravesite. The soft breeze carried with it a scent that brought him back to grade school. And even before he could see what the torches were illuminating, the evanescent beauty was gone.

It is said that smells can summon memories more powerfully than sights. This particular odor brought Jim back to the tennis courts outside the local middle school where he grew up. On Saturday afternoons the animal shelter across the street would dispose of its dead cats and dogs by incinerating the carcasses. The breeze would send the smell of the burnt flesh wafting across the tennis courts, and the sound of the yelping animals would accompany it. Jim would have to stop playing, and Matt would call him a "pansy" for not being able to take it. One time, Jim made up his mind to play through it, but then the dry heaves came on, and Matt laughed harder than ever. Jim never told Matt that it was not so much the actual smell that sickened him as the thought of what those bodies must look like as they were emitting the smell. And he never told anybody of the nightmares he used to have of shoveling living dogs into the ovens, and watching them burn alive as their yelps echoed in his ears.

He almost turned around, too frightened to face the corpses. The reek was growing stronger, and he had to stop just to prevent himself from retching. The memory of the yelping dogs was pounding his eardrums. Then he noticed those around him. None were hesitating. They saw through the stench, recognizing the brave who had died for them. These courageous warriors, who had fought to the death, were people they loved, people he could have saved. Jim walked on.

Over the hill, in the flickering torchlight he saw them: black and unrecognizable, charred arms, legs, and torsos. Some were nothing but burnt skeletons and grinning skulls, grinning accusingly at him... it was worse than his nightmares. The many who had not been reduced to mere bones stared up at him as well. As he came closer he could see their faces, trapped in tortured grimaces. They looked as though they had been carved into the charcoaled remains of a recently quenched bonfire. But they were humans, each one of them. This was evident in the way the villagers cared for the remains. There was no fear. The women helped as well, lovingly bearing the deceased heroes to their honorable graves. He was amazed. There was not one look of disgust, not one movement of apprehension. But he himself could not move. When the dirt had filled each grave, the people left to prepare for tomorrow's possible battle. Jim had not helped carry one body. He knew he must go to pray with them, for their dead. But in all his soul searching, he could not bring himself to touch those revolting mounds of roasted humanity. And when it was over, he felt as though he had failed them once again, failed those faces grimacing at him, questioning his cowardice.

He would make it up to them, to the living as well, even though none of them seemed to notice that he had remained idle. He would battle tomorrow with all his heart, to

the death if he must. When he found Samuel, he would tell
him of his resolution.

****

"NO," SAMUEL said, "that's not a good idea."

"What? But I want to; I owe it to you. I... I owe it to
my family to beat these dragons." he said, obviously flustered.

"You're just about the age when we ask our youth to
join us in battle," Samuel answered. "But you're
inexperienced. You've never seen a dragon."

"Well then, what am I supposed to do while the rest of
you defend the island?" he asked.

"I know you won't think much of it. But it's a terribly
important job. I talked to Hun Kanny about it, and he agrees:
You are to help us take care of the little ones. They need
someone to look to while they're waiting for the outcome of
the battle."

"But... I can do more than that. I've been through a
lot. I *am* experienced now. I jumped off of the bridge. I
almost drowned in the lake. I... I found Hun Kanny!" he
exclaimed.

"And thank you," Samuel interrupted, "But that is
precisely why you cannot be in the battle. Hun Kanny can
help us win this thing. But having you in the line of fire will
compromise his ability to fight. You see, he was always meant
to be your guardian. That's not the case with Calapanta." Jim

looked confused. "Can't you understand," he continued, "you come first. Protecting you will always come first to him."

Jim failed to respond.

"No. You're to stay with the children – for us *and* for your family."

Chapter Twelve

PREPARING A NEW THRONE

ONCE THE Red Dragon saw that Luntha had run the boy through, it turned and flew away. It could not understand why the boy had failed to call for his guardian. This was supposed to be the perfect plan. The boy was sure to call. There had been no doubt about that. And when Hun Kanny responded, as he most certainly would, the boy could then be used as live bait. The three dragons would defeat Hun Kanny together. But in an odd twist, the boy chose to die alone. This perplexed the Red Dragon: did it mean that his death would waken the schwah prince or would it cause him to remain in his deep slumber until the end of time? Whatever the case, no one else remained who could call upon Calapanta's protector. Perhaps the war would be won without the difficulty of facing Hun Kanny. Part of it was disappointed, for it yearned to feast upon Hun Kanny's heart. However, deep down below all the lies upon which its pride depended, it knew that Hun Kanny would be no easy foe to conquer, even if they used the schwah's own precious human to bait him into their territory. It remembered their first battle.

And so, it left. There was nothing more to see. The human clungen, one of its most effective, was now ready for the final transformation. It flew away before it could see Luntha cradling the young hero in his arms. It couldn't possibly know that it had lost what it thought it had won.

****

"HEY LOOK at me. Look, I'm Mr. Red!" One of the dragons sat on the throne in the cave. "I've got all the power. Look who's in the big seat now!" As the other dragon laughed its squeaky laugh the one on the throne grunted and gave it a kick. "Yeah, I can do whatever I want. Ooh, yeah, I'm Mr. Red; I'm Mr. Scary." It raised its hands in feigned alarm, and made a face of mocked fear. Then it pantomimed scratching the seat with its claws. "Oh, yeah, I almost forgot, I've got the cleanest seat around. Don't touch it! You'll mark it up with your dirty little claw prints." And it snorted insolently, spewing forth two great puffs of smoke upon the seat of the throne.

"Yeah! Why do we put up with this?" asked the one with the squeaky laugh. It was still cowering in the corner after the kick. "Why don't the two of us rule the lair? We could control the clungens, and they'd have to do whatever *we* told them."

"Because I would destroy you both," said a short, bald man in a navy blue suit. It, or rather *he*, had just entered the cave as the second dragon had finished its statement. The man did not appear perturbed in the least.

The first dragon jumped down from the throne, while the second one stammered, "I... I was just kidding... I... I'll always serve you, Big Red."

"I'm sure you will," he said, remaining calm. "Would you be so kind as to clean my seat? You seem to have soiled it." Then he strolled confidently passed them both.

"It may do you well to remember that it was I who freed you from the Pit of Bashaan," he continued. "You would still be wallowing in your own reek if I had not helped you. Now I won't pretend that I did it out of compassion. No, you both know too well that I don't care what happens to you after we win. I don't care at all. But just remembering Bashaan should be enough to remind you of my surpassing power. The two of you together could not escape. And those were *good* times in the Pit. Let's reminisce shall we?" Now it was his turn to do the mocking.

"No, Big Red. We don't have to," they pleaded.

"Did you say 'no'?" he continued mocking them. "I think we shall. Let's see. When I first saw you," he said, staring at the one who had been sitting on his throne, "you were... you were.... now you must jog my memory. I'm not sure if I can recall it clearly. Please tell me what was happening to you the first time I saw you." The black dragon hesitated. "Are you going to make me say 'please' twice?" He looked over his spectacles at the trembling dragon.

"I was chained to the Rock of Shame. And I was being... I was... Boss, hey boss, your seat's clean now. Come look. Here see, it's just like new... better than new, cleaner than when you first got it." It was tremulous.

"Come now. Don't insult me like this. I was the first to clean it. You mean to tell me that a dragon who was once chained to the Rock of Shame, unable to do anything about it, could possibly clean my throne better than I?" This time it was a look of playful disappointment with which he beheld the dragon.

"No, Red, I didn't mean..."

"No, you didn't," the little man interrupted. "And what about you?" He turned to the other dragon, who immediately began twitching. "No. I think that's about enough nostalgia for one evening, especially for one so abundant with good fortune." He smiled, a twinkle in his eye. "As you can see, I am ready to go back to Maine."

The mood lifted. "That means we're ready to finish the island?"

"Yes, that means the two of you can have fun preparing it for my return."

"But what about Hun Kanny? Do we have to face Hun Kanny?" The first dragon's voice shook with fear.

"You mean to tell me that two big, bad dragons like yourselves are afraid of that little schwah?" He snorted a short chuckle.

"Well, Red, if he could beat you..." The second dragon was cut short. It was thrown to the wall of the dragons' lair by an unexpected burst of flame and screeched in agony.

The burning vapor dissipated quickly. "Now that that's settled, we can continue... As I said, this evening has been just *filled* with good fortune. That means that you two cowardly lizards won't have to worry about Hun Kanny after all. To ease your mind, I'll let you know that I personally watched his maggot die. There is no one to waken him." They were indeed much relieved at this news.

He continued, "Isn't it funny, almost ironic, that a creature as powerful as Hun Kanny, that all schwahs for that matter, can be so dependent on dirt. It's downright laughable. When I think that I was told to serve those pieces of excrement... I would *rather* serve pieces of *excrement!*" he laughed.

"Yeah, Red, that's right. That's funny... 'serve pieces of excrement'... really is." And the first black dragon did his best to laugh.

"Yes, it is funny," said the little baldheaded man, "because I can be *quite* funny." The other two were not sure if they were meant to laugh at the irony of this statement. It was truly humorous, but they were too frightened of the Red Dragon to laugh *at* him. So they decided it would be safest to nod their heads in agreement.

"Yeah, Red's the funniest I ever heard," claimed the first black dragon.

"Me too," followed the other. Then it risked a suggestion. "Say, Red, what about attacking tonight? If Hun Kanny isn't around, what's to stop us from attacking tonight?" it asked.

"Because you two would fly away as soon as you were hit in the chest with their rocks. That's why," he explained. "No, you will wait until tomorrow morning, when the newest clungens will be ready to join you."

"But I almost had them beat on my own," countered the first black dragon.

A fire lit in the little man's eyes, "While you were taking your time on the island, and while you," here he turned to the other dragon, "were busy losing the other doorway we need to control, I was conquering the mainland. I will not risk any more failures. We will attack tomorrow." And just as quickly as it had ignited, the fire died down.

The Red Dragon knew full well that the two black ones could easily destroy the island. But that did him no good. He was off to Maine, and he fully expected to return by tomorrow morning. It was most undesirable for them to conquer Calapanta while he was gone. This would embolden them, which was something he wanted to avoid. Remembering his battle with Hun Kanny, he had no wish to go through something like that again. At the moment, they were easily subdued. Unable to trust them, he used fear to maintain control. As of yet, they were too afraid of the Red Dragon to disobey his commands. In fact, he was the very reason that both of them had failed earlier. He had called them back when they were on the brink of victory. He did not want them to have the experience of winning without his help.

"Yes," he smiled this time, "tomorrow will work out just about right."

With that, he left for Maine to create his new throne.

****

THE LITTLE, bald man with the navy blue suit, white dress shirt, and black wingtip shoes walked along the rooftop of Stackingsdale High, inspecting the clungens' progress. He approached one who was standing still, watching the others work feverishly. As soon as the clungen saw him approaching, it turned and bowed to him.

"I trust this will be ready by tomorrow morning," he said.

"We are working very hard," was the cautious reply.

He tilted his head and raised his eyebrows. "I shall repeat myself... I trust this *will* be ready by tomorrow morning."

The clungen bent down and picked up a whip. "Yes," it answered.

"Good... Good. It will be much appreciated. Now, I must be on my way." He then turned to leave.

Exiting the school, he walked through the somber streets of Stackingsdale, Maine, off to inspect the largest building in the city, which he had spotted the night before. It was on top of a hill on the other side of the river.

As he approached the site, he met with a group of clungens coming toward him from outside the city boundaries. They were rolling several carts filled with prisoners. The small towns surrounding Stackingsdale had now been cleared.

"I see it's going well," he said.

"Much easier than Calapanta," was the response. "They don't put up a fight."

"Wonderful." He looked in one of the caged carts. "Yes, truly wonderful." He paused for a moment. "Well, carry on. I wouldn't want to think that I had slowed you down," he said, and continued on his way.

He stood in front of the gray stone building, almost in awe. The front doors were enormous. He would be able to enter and exit as he pleased. The steeple in the front was a worthy signpost for his throne. "It's truly magnificent," he thought, "as if they were expecting me."

When he entered, he was astounded. There at the end of the long aisle was a large stone block. It would be perfect to lean his elbow against as he rested on his throne. Then there were the long seats – rows and rows of them. His slaves would fill these seats and honor him with their praise and worship. He could not have conceived a better floor plan. Pillar after pillar lined the walls to his left and to his right. It was majestic, built for a king! He could not imagine for Whom it had been made. And it was empty – just ready for him to occupy.

Truth be known, the One for Whom it was made had been removed, in a small golden box, months earlier under the pretense that "it was better that way." With the box no longer present, the building could "double" as an auditorium. There had also been various statues set up in the building, but these had been sold at auction. They were purchased by a southern tourist who, thinking they looked "quaint", bought them for a steal. He put them in his garden behind his house to give it an "old-fashioned" look, which was rather odd, because being "old-fashioned" was precisely the reason they were removed in the first place.

Thus, void of anyone to claim proprietorship, it truly was ready for him to occupy. There was only one aspect of the building that bothered him: the strange pictures on the windows. He couldn't understand them, and he hated what he couldn't understand. So he smashed them, and the grass surrounding the building was littered with the shattered paintings of heroic deeds. He then opened the door to call to a clungen.

"You will replace the broken windows with red glass," he said.

"Yes," it responded.

"It must be the same hue as my scales." The clungen gave a nod. "You do remember the color of my scales?" It nodded again. The little man continued, "This morning's sunrise is to flood the building's interior with red."

"This morning's?" the clungen spoke. "That's only a few hours away."

"Let me restate: This morning's sunrise *will* bathe my throne with red. If the sunrise does not, something else will. Do you understand?" The clungen nodded for the third time.

The little man in the navy blue suit reentered the building. He couldn't help it; not being given to temperance, he must indulge himself. He walked up the aisle, around the stone block, and sat on the cushioned seat behind it, facing the stone. He smiled. "Truly unbelievable," he said aloud. He had thought he would need to spend the night readying his throne, but in a minute's work, the only renovations necessary had begun. Clungens were cleaning the shattered glass outside and throwing it away, careful to make the area neat and tidy for their master. And red panes of glass were already on their way.

DAWN ARRIVED while he continued to sit on his throne, and, when the sun broke over the hills, he basked in the blood red light as it inundated the building, just as he had desired.

The time had come to defeat Calapanta. With his two thrones firmly set, he was anxious for his third. The island would take little more than the morning to destroy. Then he could work on the final doorway himself.

Thus far his plan was working well. He waltzed toward the high school. As he approached, he could see the bodies of several dead clungens lying at the base of the building. After casually stepping over a carcass, he opened the front door. Then he summoned a clungen to him. "I know that you will have this place cleaned up by the time I return. I don't want those things sullying my land." He flippantly waved toward the doorway with the back of his hand. The slave nodded.

He made his way to the roof and, seeing many more dead bodies, smiled and said, "I trust it is ready."

The clungen responsible for the job answered that it was ready. The doorway had been stronger than expected and the explosion much greater than anticipated, but the task was now complete. The clungen's only concern now was that the disturbance would eventually cause the doorway to shut down entirely. They would then be stuck in Maine.

"Let me worry about that," said the little man.

He knew full well that what the clungen had said was indeed a danger. But this was not a venture he had undertaken haphazardly. In fact, while in exile, he had studied the doorways quite diligently. Yes, he knew exactly how to keep it open.

"You just let *me* worry about that," he said again. And with that he walked through the doorway, which could now transport him in whichever form he chose to take.

****

THE RED Dragon stood outside the lair and blew a steady stream of fire into the cave. It could hear the squealing of the two black dragons, and it grinned.

"Come, you two," it announced. "It's time to attack." When they came out, complaining of their burns, the contrast between the dragons could easily be seen. The Red Dragon was much larger and more powerful than the two black ones. And as they slunk around it, it gloated in its superiority. "The clungens should be setting foot on the island's shores just about now. By the time we arrive, there will be little more than an aftermath to clean up." Confident in its strength and in the islanders' weakness, it would snuff out any remaining rebels with a mere puff. The time for victory had arrived. "And, I have given orders for as many prisoners to be taken as possible. The doorway must be kept open."

When the two black dragons asked what this meant, it scoffed at them: "Your ignorance is shocking at times... even if you *are* of a much lower nature. It simply boggles the mind how little the two of you comprehend concerning the secret realms." Though the Red Dragon knew that only a schwah prince had access to these realms, it still enjoyed any opportunity to demean these two.

The smaller dragons shuffled uncomfortably before one of them finally spoke. "Well, Red, we didn't..."

The Red Dragon cut in before it could finish. "It's their blood, my dears, their blood. The doorway will not go out of existence as long as fresh human blood flows through it. But without the blood – after a few more days – poof..." As it finished, it blew a light cloud of smoke that quickly disappeared. "Yes, we need plenty of humans. And we need them alive."

When it had finished its explanation, the three dragons ascended into the sky, flying across the desert, over the mountains and over the sea, to the shores of the small island that had held out against them.

Chapter Thirteen

BAD CLUNGEN, GOOD CLUNGEN

SOMEWHERE, DEEP in the jungle, a man and his wife slept soundly in their tent near the river. They had been exploring all day and were exhausted, looking forward to a good night's sleep. But it was not to be.

At two o'clock in the morning the woman woke with a start. She turned to her husband and shook him. "Jim," she said, "something's about to happen to one of our children... something dreadful." Her voice was trembling.

He didn't ask which child. And if he did, she wouldn't have been able to tell him. The husband didn't even ask how she knew. He had grown accustomed to her peculiar clairvoyant ways. He had no doubt, however, concerning the veracity of what she said. One of their children was in terrible danger, and *that* was what mattered. Their world had changed in an instant. The man grabbed his crutch and began to pack their things. But his wife soon stopped him. They would do without. It was most important that they start for home immediately.

What had been a delightful adventure just a few hours before became grueling torture. The very vines on which the man had watched his wife swing with childlike playfulness the previous evening were now prison bars impeding their way. The many miles they had enjoyed traveling and exploring with each other were now their enemy. It would take three days at the very least for them to return to the palace.

The man knew he needed to pace himself, but it was difficult. Every minute felt eternal, and he found himself paddling in a frenzy unless he focused on an even, steady motion. Meanwhile, his wife sat in the front of the canoe, a statue. Finally, she turned around and gave him a sad smile. "I guess I could help," she said, breaking her silence. Then she picked up an oar and began to paddle as well. They quickly worked themselves into a sustainable rhythm cutting through the water.

****

THE THOUGHT that Luke might be captured had passed through Kor's mind, but he couldn't take it seriously. Luke was too good to be caught. Not that he was a superior spy, or especially gifted in the art of stealth like Vort – no, he was just too good. He was simply the best person Kor knew. He would quietly do his duty, and it would get done. It didn't seem possible that an enemy so evil could capture someone so good. But time was ticking away, and he could see that even Hives looked nervous.

"If we don't hear from him by noontime," he said, "then I'm going into Calapanta." Hives agreed.

There had been an interesting turn of events since Luke left. Kor had thought that there would be a desperate struggle to protect his kingdom from the Calapantan dragon. But it simply went away. It was as if it had taken one too many arrows on the snout and had lost interest. They expected it to return at any moment, and he had guards stationed at the door, but there was nothing to fight. Some of the Impids were even speculating that the fight was over. They could not have conceived the force that was intended to beat down that door within a few hours. In fact, none of them had any idea what was happening on the other side. Kor had wanted a report from Luke before risking any more Impid lives. But Luke was not returning... and twelve noon had arrived.

Hives walked with Kor to the doorway and helped him through. Of course, he could not go with Kor. No schwah could traverse the doorway; that had been the very reason why the dragon was trying to destroy it in the first place. But remaining intact, the doorway forced Kor to leave his guardian. Neither wanted this, but they both knew it was necessary. If Kor were to help Luke, he must do it alone.

****

THE BEACH sand felt soft under Kor's feet as he walked along the shore. Although the coastline appeared to be empty, he didn't trust being in the open, so he scurried like a little sand crab toward the base of the mountains lining the coast and quickly hid behind one of the many boulders there.

Then he pondered his next move. Had he known where he was he would have darted straight up the mountainside. A path lay before him climbing some two thousand feet. If he hurried, he could reach the peak within a couple of hours. Then, going down the other side, he would have seen his brother slowly staggering across the desert. But he did not make his way up this path. Instead, he wandered about trying to decide where he should go. Soon, the sun's heat began to impress itself upon him, and he found himself hiding in the shade as much as possible. But he did not linger anywhere for too long; instead he moved from one boulder to the next searching for anything or, preferably, anyone who might provide him with some direction. Armed with his machete and protected by the large rocks on the mountainside, he thought he could surprise whomever he came upon and ask some questions, using the blade as an incentive for answers if he must.

But it was he who was surprised.

"Who are you?" came a whisper from somewhere in the rocks.

He turned to face the direction of the voice. "Kor," he answered confidently. "I've come to find my brother."

A small, blond haired girl slid out from behind a boulder not fifteen feet from him. She looked to be about ten or eleven and had all the signs of a lengthy seclusion. Her face was dusty, and her lips were blistered. But beneath her matted, knotty blond hair she had stunning blue eyes – sky blue – and staring into them was like staring into crystals. They had somehow remained unblemished by the trauma that had afflicted the rest of her emaciated body. The clothing she wore looked to be of the finest material; Kor guessed that her family must have been quite affluent. However, her garments had become torn and filthy and were now little more than rags.

"So, you're not one of *them*?" she asked, her voice barely audible.

"No, I'm not one of them," he answered. "What's been happening here?"

She stared at him silently at first. Then she blurted out, "Please help me!" and breaking down, ran up to him weeping. "My family was taken away," she cried. "All of them... It was awful." Here she looked away, as if remembering the horror of the event. Then turning back, she continued through her tears. "I just watched as I hid behind a rock." And she shivered in the heat of the sun.

"I'll try to help," he said as he reached out to hold her hand. "You see, I'm looking for my brother... and he could be with them. Where were they taken?" A breeze began blowing in from the ocean, causing a few golden strands of her unkempt hair to wisp over her ravishing blue eyes. Looking down at her, waiting for her answer, Kor thought she was the dirtiest, most beautiful little girl he had ever seen.

"Over the mountain," she replied. "I'll show you." She let go of his hand and began climbing up the path.

He followed her silently as time passed by. Conversation was not truly possible anyway. It was a steep incline, and she was moving quickly. Every so often, she would turn around to make sure he was keeping up, and then continue.

They were about half way up the path before he started to grow suspicious. He realized that he had been trusting her solely because she appeared to be desperate. And he had been a king long enough to learn that it is unwise to judge by appearances. He noticed that she had a little too much spring in her step for a girl who had been starving on the hot mountainside for the last few days. And then there were those eyes. How did they come to remain so strikingly beautiful? Should there not be some sign of strain in them – perhaps a touch bloodshot? It was as if they were intended to mesmerize. Here was this pitiful thing of a girl, and to top it off, she had eyes that could ask you to fight a lion and you would do it. It didn't make sense. And so, as the sun began setting over the mountains, he decided to test her.

"Where exactly are we going?" he asked.

"Just over the top of the mountain. You'll see," she said.

"Maybe we should take another path," he said as he came to a stop. "This one's a little too open – maybe over there." He pointed to their left where some trees were growing on the sturdy mountainside. Though they were small, they were the only living plant-life nearby.

"No, no. Please sir," she pleaded, "you don't know the way... and," she continued, "and you said you could help me get my family back." The tears that welled up in her imploring blue eyes were so heartrending that he nearly forgot his purpose. He wanted to hug her tightly and tell her that he would go wherever she led him. But he held firm.

"I know, but it seems safer over there. And there's more shade. Let's just go over there and try it out."

"No. Follow me. I know how to get there." And she tugged at his shirt. He could see that she was losing her patience and was about to break. He would soon find out what was happening.

"You go ahead, little girl," he said. "I'll catch up with you. First I want to try over here." Then he pulled himself free and made his way toward the trees, pretending to ignore her.

"Come with me!" it groaned as it charged at Kor. Kor turned, brandishing his machete, but he almost dropped it. The transformation was staggering. The little girl with the hypnotic eyes was gone, and in her place was a hooded figure, swinging a mace, which was about to crush Kor's skull. The clungen was surprised as well. It did not expect the machete, so it faltered. Taking advantage of this, Kor swung across the clungen's arm, severing it at the elbow. The clungen dropped to its knees, letting out an ear piercing shriek as the mace rolled harmlessly down the mountain, bringing the bony hand and lower arm with it. Kor then raised the machete over the screeching clungen, warning it to be quiet or it would die. The screeching turned into sobbing, and the sobbing turned into silence.

Kor continued holding his weapon over the clungen. "Where are the prisoners?" he asked.

It turned away from Kor, refusing to answer.

Kor pressed his machete against the clungen's back. "Where are they?" he repeated sternly.

"The cave," it gasped. "They are in the cave."

"And," asked Kor pushing the machete more firmly between the clungen's shoulders, "where is this cave?"

"Very far," it answered. "Over the mountains... across the Dragons' Desert."

"Show me the way," demanded Kor still wielding his machete.

The clungen slumped its head forward before slowly turning to face Kor. "No," it said. "Even if you kill me, it would be better than facing *them.*"

As Kor looked into the red eyes of the defeated clungen in front of him, he could see the meaning behind its words. The refusal was final. It would not guide him. Even if he forced it to lead him, he could not trust it to take him where he wanted to go.

He almost left it, knowing that it was devoid of strength, that without its weapon it was harmless. But he turned back. There was one thing more he needed to ask. It was about the girl. She was far too real, and he could not forget her enthralling eyes. He would not believe she had been a mere figment of some evil imagination.

"The girl... who was the girl you were pretending to be?" he asked.

The clungen did not answer, so he raised the machete threateningly. But his weapon was powerless to produce the desired response. The clungen only whimpered; it could not possibly answer. It was not supposed to be human anymore; it was not supposed to have feelings anymore. So it could not answer, for to answer would be to make it human again.

Kor connected the dots. "You..." And he stopped. He could feel himself on the verge of a rage. But he knew that a fit of ranting and raving, of cursing and swearing of the worst words he could think of would only lessen the evil of this despicable thing in front of him. Instead he lowered his voice, speaking through his clenched teeth, "...your own daughter..."

For some reason, this enticed the clungen to give Kor one more piece of information. "There *is* one prisoner not so far away."

It saw that it had grabbed Kor's attention. "Yes. He should be just on the other side of the mountain by now..." Then it chuckled, mocking Kor. "They are watching him die."

Again, Kor turned to leave, but then remained to ask one last question. "What were you leading me to?"

"The Red Dragon," it answered.

Kor left the clungen kneeling on the mountainside. He knew he wouldn't be followed. He was more concerned with the prisoner who was being forced across the desert. In his mind there was only one person it could be.

He began running, sprinting back to the path between the mountains. At the same time however, he could not forget the little girl who had been betrayed by her father. Those captivating eyes behind that sullied face were seared into his mind, and though he was looking at the rocks in front of him, he continued to see her eyes. Yes, he continued to see them as he pictured his brother struggling across the hot desert. How hot it was he could not have imagined. Nor could he have realized the extent of Luke's injuries. He saw those eyes, and he saw his brother straining to walk, and he ran.

****

MEMORIES FLOODED his mind as he hurried up the path – fond memories of his younger brother. But as he approached the summit, his mind brought him back much further to long forgotten memories that were not so fond.

When Kor was in fifth grade, almost three years before his parents adopted Luke, his cousin Georgie had come to visit. Until now, Kor had forgotten Luke had come as well. Kor's life had changed so drastically since then that he had completely forgotten what he had done to Luke. How could he never have apologized to his younger brother? How could Luke have forgiven him, never bringing it up? As the memory became more vivid, Kor sprinted faster; he could no longer bear it, and he wanted to forget once again, but it was a deluge that could not be wiped out. He was a rotten older brother. A real older brother would have apologized profusely the first chance he had. Had the roles been reversed, he knew that he would never have allowed Luke to forget it.

His mother was on the way out of the house when she told Kor to clean up the front yard. He was playing with Georgie in the back, so, of course, he didn't listen. After she drove away, it was Luke who cleaned the yard. He began by raking.

Georgie noticed this from the corner of the house, and raising his finger to his lips, pointed it out to Kor. Kor made his way over to where Georgie was standing. He had already forgotten that Luke was doing *his* job *for* him. Georgie whispered, "All right. On three we attack. You push him down, and I'll give him a wedgie."

He could see that Kor was hesitating. Kor had been given many wedgies by the older students at school and had not particularly cared for them. "Come on. It's only for fun," argued Georgie. "He won't even care. Luke doesn't care about anything." Why Georgie even needed Kor to join him was a mystery. He was the strongest eleven-year-old Kor knew, and Luke was undersized for his age.

Georgie looked down the street. Three junior high girls were making their way up the road which crossed the one the boys were on. "No. Let's wait until they can see it."

This new distraction caused Kor to forget his inhibitions about the idea. He ceased to think of Luke as a cousin, or even as a person. He became something with which to have fun.

"Okay... now!" The girls were in a direct line of sight with Luke. The two boys ran behind him, and Kor pushed him in the back. He could not believe it. He had pushed Luke to the ground! Tears were streaming down his face as he scrambled up the path. He didn't care who might see him now... he didn't deserve to be Luke's brother.

Yes, he pushed Luke to the ground. And Georgie ran up beside Kor and picked up Luke by his underwear. He grabbed the elastic band and yanked Luke into the air. Kor could hear the soft cloth tear as Luke hung, suspended by his brother's hand. Kor closed his eyes, as if to stop the memory. He picked up his pace, so that he could barely breathe. He did not want to remember.

And Georgie called to the girls: "Hey ladies!" They looked over and started laughing. Unlike Kor, Georgie was comfortable talking to girls – even older girls. "Hey ladies!" he said again. "What do you think of this hottie?" And he bounced Luke up and down. The elastic band had separated itself from the cloth by now. The girls thought it was the funniest thing they had ever seen. They could be heard giggling down the street as they disappeared behind the trees. Then Georgie, chuckling quite heartily himself, dropped Luke on the ground. He turned to Kor and said, "I'm so happy my parents adopted him. He's a lot of fun."

Luke had not screamed. He had not resisted, nor did he complain once it was over. He rose to his feet and continued raking the leaves.

"See, I told you he wouldn't care," said Georgie. And Kor bought it. He bought it! He had made himself believe that it was possible to do something like this to another human, and it was acceptable. Kor had not partaken in such cruelty before or since. Within a few days he had forgotten all about it. Somehow he had managed to rationalize the incident away. In a few months he had forgotten that Luke had even come with Georgie.

"And he was doing *my* chores!" thought Kor as he reached the summit and started down the other side. "He was doing my chores... And I hated that thing back there. That thing that used to be a father." And the eyes that had been seared into his mind were blaming *him* now.

****

HE FINALLY stopped, leaning against a rock to breathe. He excused the halt by looking out over the desert. Though the moon was shining down brightly, it was still too dark to see very far, so he strained his eyes to observe any movement over the open plain in front of him.

Then he heard it. It was a gentle sobbing close by. He looked around, but was unprepared for what he saw when he located the source of the sound.

There was a man, sitting on the ground, holding something in his arms. He was wearing a cloak, but the hood was pulled back, and his face was bent over the object he cradled. Kor walked over to him, but before the man noticed he was there, he saw that the object was a boy. And through the swollen cheeks, and bloated lips, he could see Luke. He could see him through his empty, dead eyes, staring up at the cold stars above.

The lance was still protruding from Luke's chest, and the blood, running over the man's lap, had formed a puddle beside a rock.

Kor sat down beside the man, and pulling Luke out of his arms, he held his brother close. Kor was now sobbing as well. He stared into the night sky and moaned. "Why!" he yelled. "Why!... He doesn't deserve..." He stopped, too choked up to speak. His shoulders shook up and down in small spasms as he wept. Then he looked at the man: "Who did this?" he managed through the tears.

"I did." The man continued to sit. Kor shot to his feet, letting the limp body fall to the ground. He gripped his machete and swung it toward the man's neck, intending to decapitate him. The man sat still, staring at Luke's body. The blade stopped half an inch short of Luntha's unflinching neck. Kor stumbled backwards. The man sat there, defenseless, as he continued to stare at the corpse, and Kor had almost beheaded him. Murder was not the answer. Adding evil to evil would not bring his brother back.

"How could you..." he wept. "He was my..." and he couldn't go on. He looked down at the body on the ground and grabbed the lance, dislodging it from his brother and throwing it aside. He scooped Luke into his arms and sat down again. "I'm sorry," he cried. "I'm sorry. I should have gone, not you. I should have been killed. I'm sorry for everything." Then he went quiet and squeezed Luke close to his chest, rocking back and forth on the mountainside.

They were both silent. Finally, he looked at Luntha. "I'm not burying him here," he said. "I need to bring him home."

Luntha rose to his feet. "I'll carry him," he said. He hoisted Luke's body across his shoulders and followed Kor over the path to the beach. It took several hours, but in that time, there was no speaking. Luntha carried the body, and Kor led the way. Kor continued on mechanically, but his brain had shut down. He could not think; his whole being had gone numb in a walking stupor.

When he passed through the doorway, his parents were there. Before they could greet him, they saw Luntha with Luke on his shoulders, and, reaching for their dead son, they held him. They didn't ask why or how. They simply held him. Tears streamed down their faces, but there was no wailing or sobbing. And they quietly carried him to the church where they covered him with a shroud. This was where he would remain until his casket arrived the next day.

Hives had waited in the background until Kor's parents walked away. Kor knew that they must be with Luke, and that they could not console him now. But when his schwah put an arm lovingly around him, he broke down sobbing once more. Hives let him cry, holding him close. Until this moment Kor hadn't realized how desperately he had needed to let his emotions out. And he wept without restraint as he buried himself in his friend's arms.

WHEN KOR was able to regain his composure, he started to the church. It was a slow walk, and once there he sat in the last pew. He was a zombie, not wanting to talk, not wanting to sleep – incapable of sleep. Whenever he closed his eyes to rest he saw Luke's dead body. Behind it was the blond girl's dirty face, and her sad, piercing eyes continued to blame him. Then he would open his eyes and stare at the crucifix in the front of the church. Once, he turned around to see if Hives was there. The schwah was standing motionless in front of the doors, and *his* stare was fixed on the same crucifix. The representation of the man nailed to a cross consumed his attention; he didn't notice that Kor was looking back at him. Kor turned around to face the front of the church again. He knew that nothing, not even Hives, could comfort him now except that man on that cross. So he faced forward and meditated on Him.

His parents were sitting in the front, his father's crutch leaning against the pew. Luntha was in the aisle next to them. Just before sunrise, Kor's mother stood up and walked over to her son's killer. "It was a good death," she said. Knowing that she was not asking a question, he nodded his head in agreement.

****

THE SUN had long since risen when Kor left the church, but it was not yet noon. His father and mother would stay there in mourning, but he could not. And as much as his parents hated to see him go, they too knew he couldn't stay. Like so many good kings, he must put his misery second, and put his subjects first. And the time had come for him to lead his Impids into battle.

The father greatly desired to join Kor, to battle the dragon next to his son; but his wife held his arm and, without speaking, let him know that this was not a battle he could fight... at least, not in person. The two of them would be of far more use if they remained in the church, praying. And so they said good-bye to Kor, trusting in God to carry *this* son through the "valley of death" he was about to enter.

Kor met with Luntha to discuss the situation in Calapanta. He was told of the Red Dragon's ultimate plan of destroying the Impids' doorway and conquering the Amazon. Kor felt that it made more sense to surprise them in Maine, or even in Calapanta, than to wait for the attack in the jungle. Hives reluctantly agreed that this was the better plan. Once again, he would not be there to protect Kor. In the end, they decided upon entering Maine and battling the clungens who were there. Kor had learned from the clungen he had met on the mountainside that the dragons' slaves worked through deception and fear. They were unused to any real fighting, to facing weapons that could do them harm. Bravery was not their strong point. Though the Impids were not known for their physical strength, they *were* known for their skill with the bow. And they were brave. If he could rally his warriors, he was sure they could defeat the clungens. Then, if the dragons did not enter Maine, they would surprise them in Calapanta. However, he was not as confident that they could defeat the dragons, especially without Hives. But a surprise attack offered a better chance of success than waiting in the Amazon. And then there was the fact, supplied by Luntha, that the dragons thought Jim was dead. No one in the Amazon knew where Jim was, but, until his death was confirmed, there remained the hope that Hun Kanny might yet do battle with the dragons.

While Kor explained the plan to the Impids, Luntha stood silently by his side. The mention of the clungen Kor had met interested him greatly, and he was tempted to ask Kor about it. However, he felt that after what he had done to Luke, he was the least of the warriors, and therefore, should not delay the plan; he said nothing.

When Kor had finished talking, he turned to Luntha. "Who would know that you left?" he asked.

"No one," said Luntha. Then he paused and, looking down, shook his head slowly. "It wouldn't cross their minds that I could."

Kor pressed him no further. "Good, that works in our favor. When we enter Maine, you need to separate from us and pretend you're still a clungen." Luntha agreed; then pulling his hood back over his head, he hid his face.

There were no more preparations to be made. The time had come. Kor gathered his Impid army and headed for the doorway to Maine.

PART IV

AT THE WATER'S EDGE

Have mercy on me, O God, in your faithful love,
in your great tenderness wipe away my offences;
wash me thoroughly from my guilt,
purify me from my sin.

For I am well aware of my offences,
my sin is constantly in mind.
Against you, you alone, I have sinned,
I have done what you see to be wrong,

that you may show your saving justice when you pass sentence,
and your victory may appear when you give judgment,
remember, I was born guilty,
a sinner from the moment of conception.

But you delight in sincerity of heart,
and in secret you teach me wisdom.
Purify me with hyssop till I am clean,
wash me till I am whiter than snow.
(Psalm 51:1-7)

Chapter Fourteen

LEAVING THE BASEMENT

DAWN ARRIVED. Samuel had been working through the night. He encouraged the other islanders to rest, but he could not. Neither could Jim. He followed Samuel around as the preparations were being made, obsequiously doing whatever he was asked, hoping that Samuel would change his mind. If Samuel could only see how useful he was, then he might turn to Jim and say, "You know what? I've thought it over, and we could really use you." But he didn't. Instead Samuel begged him to take a nap. Jim claimed not to be tired and then left to try his luck with Hun Kanny. The schwah was busily tearing down trees to make more weapons when Jim approached him and asked if it would be possible for him to join in the battle. Hun Kanny simply pointed toward Samuel and carried on with his work.

Behind Samuel, Jim could see the women busy with their preparations. They were taking great care to ensure that the children would be comfortable, that their little minds would be at peace, as far away from the battle as possible. They were the treasure of the people, and their safety was top priority. The defense was arranged so that the last place to fall would be the village itself. If that occurred, the basements the islanders had built would be difficult to discover. Each was a well-designed place of refuge – safe-havens in the midst of battle. They had no visible openings, the windows having been camouflaged by wooden boards covered with dirt and grass. Jim's heart sank when he thought of being treated like a helpless child, shut up inside while others were defending the island. It was his duty, he decided, to help them fight. He would confront Samuel again, and this time he would not give up.

But then the sun rose, and Samuel was called away. The rays enveloped the island, but the sun itself was still hidden behind the sharp mountains surrounding the village. Jim looked up to see the crags against the sunrise. One particular summit stood out. There appeared to be a boulder resting on its peak. It was oddly balanced, and he wondered how it remained affixed to the tiny point beneath. The rock itself must have been enormous to be so distinct from this distance. And the connection to the rest of the mountain looked slight. "It's got to fall sometime soon," he thought, and he moved to find a better angle from which to view the oddity. In so doing he left the boulder's shadow and was blinded by the sun, which, by this time, had risen between the mountaintops. As he shut his eyes and turned away, Samuel reentered the village. A lookout had spotted the clungens on the ocean. Hundreds, maybe thousands, could be seen coming over the western horizon. They were still too far away for an accurate count, but there was no doubt: the battle was about to begin.

Most of the warriors, having already received their instructions, ran into the mountains. Others made their way to Hummingbird Lake, this being of special significance for them as well as for the Red Dragon. A few more men were stationed around the village. In the event that the outer defense should fall, they would be joined by the retreating forces. Hun Kanny, however, disappeared. Samuel was the only one who knew where he went. The islanders must hold off the clungens without his help until the dragons arrived. They were to fly onto the island ignorant of his presence.

During all the commotion Jim was whisked off to safety with the other noncombatants.

****

THE CHILDREN had been separated into groups of fifteen and were sent into the various underground basements. The women were left to look after them. It didn't take Jim long to discover that he was the oldest one there. Any male eighteen years of age or older was expected to help defend the island. Those fifteen to seventeen were given the option to join if they so desired; none had refused.

Here he was, the oldest of fifteen boys, hiding in a basement like a baby. Peter came over with Tommy Tripp and a couple of the other boys, wanting to talk to him, but he told them to leave him alone. He sat on the ground next to the wall and buried his head between his knees.

"I can't believe it," he muttered, "the last one on the fence... again." He was remembering his grade school days, particularly third and fourth grade, when the morning kickball games would leave him lingering on the fence. This was two or three years before hockey. Back then, even the younger students were picked before he was. And there never seemed to be an even number of players. He was the proverbial "odd man out". The football games during recess and the basketball games after school resulted in the same outcome. He had forgotten the feeling... until now.

He was a loser again.

When Peter came back and sat next to him, he grunted.

The nine year old looked up at him. "Hey, thanks for bringing Hun Kanny back to us," he said.

Jim couldn't respond; he stood up and walked away. He knew he needed to do something. Being trapped in this basement was sickening. He could hear Matt Pierce calling him a "pansy" once more.

A mist coated Peter's eyes, as he sat dejected in the corner. He didn't know what he had done, but he knew he must have done *something* in order for Jim to treat him this way. He had spent yesterday evening bragging to Tommy and the others that he was friends with the boy who had brought back Hun Kanny. He told them that he would make sure they were put in his basement, so they could meet the new hero. When Jim told them to go away, it was embarrassing, but Peter blamed it on the possibility that Jim was not in the mood to meet his friends. It was a much bigger blow when he grunted and walked away. Peter had nothing else to blame it on and felt rejected. He sat in the corner crying quietly.

Meanwhile, Jim was looking around the room. He nervously tapped his leg, convincing himself that he needed to escape. "I risked my life on the bridge," he thought. "And I risked it again in the cave." Then he noticed that the locks to the windows were within his reach. "I need to be out there fighting dragons," he concluded, arguing with the wall behind him.

When he walked over to the window, he noticed Peter. The boy had his head buried between his knees, just as Jim had a few minutes earlier, and he was mumbling softly to himself. Jim couldn't ignore him anymore.

"Hey, Pete," he said as he sat next to him. Peter looked up and smiled through his tears. He quickly wiped them off his face with his arm. "I'm sorry. I didn't mean anything by that. Just forget it, okay?" He sat with his hands folded in front of his knees, looking at Peter. Peter was sitting the same way.

"Yeah, sure,... okay," answered Peter. He was still smiling and his excited eyes were staring up at Jim.

"It's just that I don't belong down here," Jim explained. "I should be out there fighting."

"Then why aren't you?" asked Peter, ignorant of his father's command.

"Good question," said Jim. He looked down and spoke with an air of confidentiality. "Hey, if you and the other boys can promise to keep on playing just like you've been doing, while I sneak out the window, the moms in the other room won't notice I'm gone." He slowly began to smile, "Then I can do something instead of doing nothing." He patted Peter on the back. "You can do that for me, can't you?

Tell the other boys that I need to sneak out, and I need their help."

"Yeah, sure!" said Peter. Then he made his way around the room, whispering to the boys and pointing back at Jim as he explained the plan to them. There is nothing like being part of a secret to grab a boy's attention. They began playing a touch louder than they had been, but Jim felt it would do. He opened the window and pushed out the wooden board; then he climbed through. He crawled over the wood and turned around to place it back against the window, but before he did, he mouthed "Thank you" to Peter, who waved back at him. He pushed the dirt and the branches that had been disturbed back into place and slipped away. Knowing that Samuel was fighting on the coast, Jim headed for Hummingbird Lake.

****

THE BATTLE had been progressing better than expected. When the clungens reached the shore, it looked empty. They made their way inland and were attacked from behind by the islanders who had been hiding in the mountains. The Calapantans were outnumbered, but they were also invisible. They knew the island well, and Samuel had taken great pains to impress upon them the importance of staying out of sight. "Each life matters," he had said, "We can't afford anyone to be careless with his own." And as more clungens arrived, they were quickly swallowed into this fight against an invisible foe.

The dragons then appeared on the horizon, all three of them. The enormous red one was in the middle, flanked by the smaller black ones. The islanders could see them approaching across the clear blue sky, and their knees went weak. Samuel had warned them that this would happen. He had been emphatic about the dragons' greatest weapon: "Fear," he had said, "They will attempt to defeat us with fear. They will look invincible... indomitable. So do not stare at them any more than you must; it will only lure you into despair. If we hold fast, we can defeat them. Remember, we are not fighting alone. Hun Kanny defeated the Red Dragon before; he will do it again!" And the men had cheered. Now, gaping at these mighty creatures flying toward them, they could not quite remember why they had cheered with such confidence. But they remembered Samuel's words, and weak kneed or not, they refused to be baited into despair; they looked to their task at hand and held fast.

The Red Dragon lit up the forest as it passed by but did not stop. The black ones followed with blasts of their own. They, however, remained on the coast to battle the first line of defense. The Red Dragon was headed for Hummingbird Lake.

Upon its approach, it was bombarded by rocks. Large boulders were slung at it from all sides. It reeled back, turned and flew up toward the sun. When it had become little more than a speck in the sun's face, it turned and plunged downward. By the time it was within range it was moving too fast for them to take aim. Before it hit the water it shot toward the shore, blowing fire at the hidden islanders on the hills.

Then came the surprise. As it darted across the lake, it was struck on its side. Hun Kanny had exploded out of the water, colliding with the dragon. The two spun down into the lake, disappearing beneath the surface.

Jim broke through the trees and stared into the troubled waters of the lake, not knowing what had occurred. Meanwhile beneath the surface, a violent battle was raging. The dragon managed to free itself and burst forth from the lake. Jim was spellbound. It was greater than he had imagined. First its head appeared, fierce and powerful, emerging from the water as a great pagan god. The reptilian eyes of the red beast looked to the sky, and fire spewed forth from its nostrils. Its bloody scales coated its flesh in what appeared to be impenetrable armor. And the sharp, menacing teeth in its mighty jaws could, with one bite, tear through a grown man.

When the monster arose from the lake in its full grandeur, Jim remained exposed, gazing in awe at this demonic vision. Its mighty wings, larger than the trees behind him, were of a deep red, almost black, and they carried the hefty dragon with ease, leaving the treacherous claws at the end of its brawny arms and legs free to clutch whatever lay in their path. Finally its giant, serpentine tail whipped forcefully behind it, ready to level the forest over which it flew. But it did no damage to the island. Instead, it hastened back up to the sky, pursued by Hun Kanny. Jim hardly noticed his guardian, who was chasing the Red Dragon like a swallow attacking a crow. And, like the crow, the dragon was fleeing. But Jim remained fixated on the intimidating majesty of the red beast. The two rose into the great blue veil above, and then descended once again, Hun Kanny closing in on his enemy.

But then he saw Jim and momentarily faltered. The dragon sensed this slight change in his attack, and looked to Hummingbird Lake. There stood the boy, awestruck in his peril; too frightened to run... it became a race. As they closed in on the target, the red beast began to understand. It could not explain how they had captured the wrong human, but, grasping the present situation, it quickly deduced that the boy they had watched die in the desert was not Hun Kanny's. The schwah's presence on the island was no longer a riddle. Winning the race, the Red Dragon wrapped its tail around the boy and flew away. As it passed the surrounding mountains it called to the black dragons to join it.

It was tempted to crush the boy and then to watch Hun Kanny try to catch his pulverized body before it sank into the ocean. Then the beast thought better of it. As long as it held the boy captive, Hun Kanny could not attack. The red beast chortled as it thought about how pitiful Hun Kanny was: he would not risk the life of such an insignificant creature. The schwah prince was weak, and would be led like a puppy dog across the desert and through the doorway into Maine.

Sensing victory, it yelled all manner of obscenities at the black ones, threatening them with the hellish consequences if they failed to keep up. The sight of Hun Kanny behind them accompanied by the lashing they were receiving from their master's tongue hastened them onward at a breathless pace. Thus motivated, they arrived at the doorway ahead of the schwah. Meanwhile, Hun Kanny, who could have flown much faster but knew that if he closed in on them it could mean the boy's death, followed behind trying to conceive some way of saving Jim.

But the Red Dragon had already thought of a way. It led the black ones into Maine and hovered near the doorway waiting for Hun Kanny. All three waited, while Jim hung entwined in the beast's tail. The dragon appeared to have forgotten him. Then as Hun Kanny burst through the doorway, the red beast lashed its tail toward him presenting the boy to his protector. It began to squeeze slowly, so that Jim's grunts of pain could be clearly heard.

"Lie down on the roof, and I will let the boy free," it demanded. Hun Kanny pointed to the dragon's tail and then to the ground. "I forgot," said the beast. "You can't talk. None of your kind can! How pathetic!" it snorted a quick laugh. "You want me to free him first? Fair enough, I put him down, while the black dragons watch him, and you lie on the roof." And it placed Jim on the grass next to the school. Hun Kanny did as he was asked, and the Red Dragon immediately inflamed him with its fiery breath. The two others joined in, and the schwah prince was blown off the roof and onto the ground. The mighty dragon lifted his burning body with one paw, and threw him into the air. Before he could land, he was caught in three streams of fire, the powerful flames blowing Hun Kanny up into the air, and over the bridge.

Jim did not stay to watch. The three dragons had forgotten about him, and none of the clungens were watching him either. They were too enthralled by the spectacle in the air. So he left running – mindlessly running into the forest, which led outside the city. The branches whipped his face and arms, and thorns tore at his legs, but he did not slow down. He continued sprinting deeper into the woodland. Somewhere in his subconscious he knew where he was headed, but he did not actively think it. He was no longer paralyzed with fear; no, he was now driven by it.

****

THE DRAGONS had blown Hun Kanny hundreds of feet into the air before they stopped this second assault. Then they waited as his body fell limply to the earth. He dropped, accelerating until his black corpse, barely missing the bridge, splashed through the shallow flowing water and crashed into the riverbed. The three dragons leaped in to tear out his heart.

It was over... or so it seemed. When they entered the river he was no longer there.

This left them baffled. Having had no relationship with a human, they knew nothing of the individual doorways. They could not have known that Jim had a secret passage to Calapanta nor could they have known that his door would also be Hun Kanny's. This apparent vanishing act enraged the Red Dragon. "Where's the boy?" it demanded. Nobody knew the answer. In the fiery tantrum that followed, it burned the banks of the river until the vegetation was reduced to ash. Unsatisfied, it continued its mindless rampage, setting ablaze whatever lay within its reach. It was only after many of its clungens lay dead on the blackened earth and the houses nearest the river were enveloped in flames that its anger began to simmer. It must think of what to do next.

"We must finish Calapanta now!" it concluded. It sent the two black dragons back to destroy the island. The Red Dragon itself remained. It *must* find the schwah and kill him while he was weak. The beast did not fully realize until that moment how deeply it yearned to destroy Hun Kanny. Hatred so possessed it that it was determined to reach into the prince's chest and brutally rip out his heart. Then it would force the boy to watch as it sat on its throne and squeezed out every drop of blood, painting the large stone block red. Finally, the demonic beast would complete its victory by feasting on its prize.

Centuries of spite had culminated into this single plan to taste revenge. And just when it was about to come to fruition, the body had inexplicably disappeared. The propinquity of success... No! It would not lose again – it would have its prize! It called the clungens together and ordered them to search the area until they found the boy.

Then, consumed by its malicious obsession, the Red Dragon began its own search for Hun Kanny.

Chapter Fifteen

THE STONE BRIDGE

JIM BURST through the woods and onto the path. He slowed as he approached the small stone bridge. When it came into view, he felt safe. It was an irrational sense of safety, he knew, but he could not help thinking of the forest trees as worthy sentinels watching over him. This place meant happiness and protection, and he needed that now.

Jim's father used to take his brother and him here when they were still in grade school. The two boys would sit on the quaint little bridge and listen as their father told them stories. They would laugh at his tall tales, and tell stories of their own. Then he would ask them about school, or friends, or anything else in their lives. But the questions were never important. They were the trivial kind, the kind Jim loved to answer because he knew his father was interested in him, and not in the school or the friends or in anything else. Eventually, the talking would end, and the two boys would throw rocks into the brook below. It was small, no more than a rivulet streaming through the cracks of a dam roughly forty yards away. Finally, when they grew tired of throwing, they would look for bugs to feed the spiders. The two enjoyed throwing mosquitoes or flies or some other bothersome insect into a web and watching until the spider sprang onto her victim and wrapped it into a neat little package. And their father would laugh his contagious laugh whenever they yelled, "She got it!"

But now there was no father or brother. If they weren't dead yet, he thought, they would be soon. He was alone, and he had failed. When he arrived at the bridge, he could not make himself cross it. Standing still, he stared at the forest trees that lined the rutty banks of the stream, their strangely contorted branches all twisting and struggling to reach the sky.

He decided to go down to the water, carefully negotiating the rootage. When he reached the bottom, he stood on one of the stones protruding from the shallow brook. From this vantage point the scenery was more picturesque than he had remembered.

In fact, it was almost too picturesque to be real. This little bit of tranquility shouldn't exist anymore. It should have been obliterated along with the city... totally effaced from this sorrow-ridden land. But it was not.

He looked up the brook to the rustic, old dam. It was timeworn, wrinkled with age, but not yet ready to burst. The water spouting through the cracks was merely a testament to its duty. From this barrier the stream ran over and around the stones in its path, down under the arch of the bridge and past Jim. Here, steppingstones leading up the opposite bank next to the bridge held his attention. They were natural steppingstones, smoothed by the water that thinly coated them as it flowed down in soft blankets until it reached the stream. They were the image of "peace" he thought, a picture likely to be found on an inspirational calendar.

A slight movement in the water below distracted him from his thoughts. A baby turtle was hiding behind the stone under his feet. And he didn't know why it should be hiding in a place like this. Then looking upward, between the branches, he saw the clear September sky and guessed why it was hiding. "Afraid a bird's gonna get ya, huh?" he said, speaking down to the turtle. Then he remembered his own fear. He wasn't so different from the turtle, he thought, as he turned to look downstream.

The water continued flowing slowly past him and down the gentle slope. In some spots, the brook fell in a cascade of two and three foot drops. Nothing that resembled a cataract, but this was as violent as the little brook could manage. Other descents were more gradual. One, surrounded by protruding rocks, forced two currents to run together. This peaceful little convergence captivated his thoughts for a few seconds. The interwoven wimples of the surface appeared stationary. They were a well-knit fabric to cover the harmless stone below. Yet the water itself, which was carried along these ripples, continued on to create tiny, almost imperceptible eddies at the bottom. In the distance he saw a small basin collecting the water. The sunshine, reflecting off the basin, sent waves of light shimmering across the undersides of the leaves which canopied the little pool.

He found it strange that he had no memory of such tranquility – it was too perfect. And he walked up the slope to the dam. How does one react when put to the test and failing? For he was certain he had failed in every aspect. He thought about his faith as he made his way out onto the dam. At the moment not much made sense, but he could not ignore the serenity hidden within the forest. He looked out over the other side of the dam to see that the peaceful calm extended there as well. The sun sprinkled the diminutive lake with a thousand brilliant specks of light, some so bright that he squinted to look at them. The island in Calapanta had breathtaking beauty, he thought, but this place had peace. "Why?" he questioned. "Why is this place so peaceful today?" He looked to the silent sky for the answer.

Before he could ponder his question much further, the lake was disturbed. Something was breaking through the surface. Startled, he scurried off the dam and hid behind the trees. Peering through the branches, he couldn't make out what manner of creature it was. Then, slowly, he began to recognize *who* it was.

Kor emerged from the lake. Reaching the tree line, he turned and waited for his entire Impid army to come forth. Jim could see as he watched their resolute faces appearing out of the ripples in the water that they were disciplined. They were experienced in battle and were determined to face their enemy. In short, they were everything he had turned out not to be, and he moved back, causing a rustle in the leaves.

Kor looked over, disinterested at first, as if expecting to see a deer or a raccoon. And when he saw Jim through the branches, his head turned quizzically to one side. At first he could make no sense of it and needed time to adjust. Then realizing the full significance of what he saw, he hurried across the dam. Jim was alive! This meant Hun Kanny would defeat the dragons! He was ecstatic. But as he approached Jim there was something unsettling in the boy's demeanor, and Kor slowed down.

Jim wanted to hide away – to cower behind a tree. He simply couldn't face Kor now. And when Kor asked him what he was doing there, Jim felt shamefully naked.

KOR DIDN'T know what to make of Jim's silence. So telling him to wait there, he went back to his army. He then called Luntha aside to make certain he knew his way to Stackingsdale.

Jim looked on, perplexed. Kor appeared to be conversing with the enemy.

When they finished, Luntha hurried off into the forest, and Kor walked over to Jim. "Don't worry," he said, noticing the apprehension in Jim's face. "He's on our side. We're giving him time to infiltrate the enemy. Then we're going to attack."

"It's over" was all Jim managed to say in return.

Kor blinked his eyes in confusion, "What do you mean 'over'?"

"Hun Kanny's dead... I led him here, and they killed him." Jim's face was blank. Despair was setting in.

This time, Kor was silent. Jim stared out over the pond; his next statement was metaphysical: "Why would God let this happen?"

"Don't go there," Kor answered quickly, bringing Jim back down to earth. "It sounds like you're the one responsible, not God."

Jim was surprised by the curt response. Kor continued. "I've been through too much to waste time blaming God. That's all it is... a waste!" He turned away from

Jim in disgust, then, looking back at him, pointed a finger squarely at his chest. "I've fought through several battles over the last couple of years, and I've been tempted to despair at times, but I managed to hold on. No! I've learned that it's times like this when God's the *only* thing that makes sense. So stop whining and do what you need to." He paused for a moment before finishing. "Now, if Hun Kanny's dead, like you say, then we're going to have to fight even harder."

Jim's face remained blank as he continued staring out over the pond. "But we're just going to die."

"Which is exactly what will happen if we *don't* fight." Kor was growing impatient. "I just lost my brother, and, to be honest, getting the chance to join him doesn't sound so bad." Immediately Jim thought of Pauly and turned to look Kor in the face, but he didn't know what to say.

Kor noticed the change and debated whether he should tell Jim that Luke had died for him. He thought maybe this would shake Jim from his self-absorption. In the end, he decided it would be imprudent. "But I can't give up. Yes, we may lose, we may all be burned alive for all I know, but we can't give up."

He turned to the Impids patiently waiting behind him. "It's time to go," he said. They started their march toward Stackingsdale. Jim took a few steps with them, then stopped, and retreated back to the dam. Kor looked over his shoulder at him: "Still stuck at the water's edge..." Then shaking his head, he turned and continued to lead his army away from the dam. They made their way to the outskirts of town where they hid amongst the trees, waiting for night.

Chapter Sixteen

THE BLACK BEAST

THE DRAGONS' abrupt departure left the islanders guessing as to what had just happened. The assumption was that their fear of Hun Kanny had been the cause. And so the islanders had cheered as they watched him fly out across the ocean.

No one knew what the Red Dragon held coiled within its tail.

The clungens were confused as well. With the fleeing of the dragons they had been left to their own devices, and Samuel had already told his fighters to show no mercy; these things were no longer human.

The battle was quick and the victory complete. A few of the clungens did, however, manage to escape fleeing on their boats, and the islanders could only watch as they disappeared over the horizon toward the mainland.

With the battle over, Samuel ordered lookouts to remain on the coast; he then returned to the village. The women had already been told that the island was safe once again and that the basements could be opened. The children screamed, shouting for joy, dancing victory dances, some already reenacting the battle, concocting the events in their young imaginations.

Samuel noticed that Peter was a bit more reserved in his celebration. Though he was smiling at the other children, it was an anxious smile; he wasn't joining them in their cheers for Hun Kanny either. Rather, he appeared to be looking for something.

When he picked up Peter to give him a huge, fatherly bear hug, he was thinking of throwing rocks down by the lake. But before he could speak, he was disheartened by the question Peter asked: "Have you seen Jim?"

He quickly put his son back on the ground. "What do you mean?"

"Jim left to go help with the battle... He snuck out through the window." As Peter spoke, he could see his father's growing concern.

"Why didn't you tell anyone? Why didn't you stop him?" he questioned.

"I..." Peter's voice was barely audible. "I helped him get out."

Samuel almost lost control. On the verge of unleashing a trail of invectives, he checked himself before saying anything he would regret later. "Where did he plan to go?" he managed to ask, feigning calmness.

"I don't know. He just said that he needed to fight." Peter's answer was calm as well. His father's voice had comforted him. But the comfort was to be short-lived.

Rumors began to circulate about something that was picked up by the Red Dragon. Yes, it was almost certain that before it fled, it had grabbed an object from the shore of the lake. And Jim was nowhere to be found. One of the islanders who had been stationed at Hummingbird Lake thought he had seen the beast snatch up someone, though he wasn't sure. Samuel was having difficulty maintaining control. The emotions on the island, which had been strained over the past few days, were now on a roller coaster threatening to derail. Then came the shouts of terrified voices. Something large and grotesque had just floated to the surface of Hummingbird Lake. Those who had lingered near the lake after the battle sprinted to the village to convey the news. Samuel knew that the only way he could quell the rising fear was by remaining calm himself. Inside he felt the panic mounting. The thought that Jim had been captured by the Red Dragon was becoming more a concrete reality than conjecture. And if this thing in the lake was what he thought it was, then he could be confident that he knew why the beast had captured Jim. His heartbeat quickened, but he controlled his shaking voice as he asked that several of the island warriors accompany him to the lake. His calm demeanor gave the villagers a sense of confidence yet again. Following his lead, they did not allow the growing fear to result in bedlam.

When they arrived at Hummingbird Lake, Samuel immediately recognized Hun Kanny's charred body. Suspecting this from the moment he heard the news, he had prepared himself for the sight. The others, still forcing themselves to follow their leader, helped him drag the blackened body ashore. Hun Kanny was as still as a corpse, but when Samuel pressed his ear against the schwah's chest he could hear a faint heartbeat. It was slow and irregular, but still there.

The men worked together to carry the schwah to the village. Samuel had sent a messenger ahead for preparations to be made. The children were immediately taken back into hiding. Samuel could not imagine that the dragons would allow Hun Kanny to live when they had been able to weaken him so.

A bedding of leaves covered with soft blankets had already been made by the time the men arrived. Within minutes, they had laid the schwah prince down onto his makeshift bed. It was not long before he moved. When he opened his eyes, the islanders experienced a sense of relief. But only a sense, for they could see what the schwah was trying to do. Attempting to stand, he could do no more than rock his head forward. His healing power was working, but it was not instantaneous.

Then came the news of the approaching dragons. There were only the two black ones, but with Hun Kanny out of commission, they would surely destroy the island. The mountains surrounding the village were still smoldering from earlier that day, and it would not take long for the dragons to have them blazing again.

Hun Kanny beat his wings furiously. He was far from flourishing, but he felt his strength returning with each stroke. Finally, he managed to raise himself off the ground just as the dragons had reached the shore. They wasted no time with the forest, but rather headed straight for the village. Before they arrived they saw Hun Kanny hovering, waiting for them. The effect of this menacing black beast in front of them, blowing fire in their direction, was terrifying. But it was not enough to frighten them away. The thought of returning to the Red

Dragon without having conquered the island evoked even more fear. So they cautiously battled the unrecognized black thing until they found that they were stronger than it was. With this realization, they soon had it overpowered, and it fled toward Hummingbird Lake. But this was no mindless flight from danger. Hun Kanny knew they would chase him. He was merely buying time.

The two dragons, aware they could destroy him and then the island, were anxious in their pursuit. But it was in vain that they tried to catch him. He was too fast. And as he dove in and out of the water his strength continued to return. If he could only evade them for a little while longer, he would then be strong enough to drive them away. But before he was ready, the dragons unexpectedly changed tactics. They began working together. One dove into the water chasing the schwah prince, while the other hovered over the lake waiting for him to reemerge. When he did, he was caught by surprise. The dragon hovering over the water flew into him, pinning him to the shore. It went straight for his heart. But as its jaws compressed around the schwah's chest, it felt something strike its eye. At first it didn't know what had happened. As the pain increased, it realized that the object had penetrated its cornea, blinding that eye. The pain continued to build until it was unbearable, and it unconsciously let Hun Kanny loose. Meanwhile, it could feel itself being pelted. When it looked over to see what was happening, another projectile, blunt and hard, struck the bone just above its good eye. Quickly squeezing its eyelid shut, it flew up and away from the lake. The other dragon, unable to locate the islanders hiding amongst the trees, blew flames at the trees themselves, attempting to stop the ceaseless barrage.

With one dragon blindly flying into the sky and the other busy with the villagers, Hun Kanny stood up. This time when he took flight, he was confident he could overpower them. As he rose higher and higher, the dragon followed, until he stopped, and the two beasts, the one blackened by fire and the other by evil, hovered hundreds of feet above the island facing each other, their wings beating the air with rapid figure eight motions. The aerial face-off lasted no more than a second. There were no blows. The dragon, sensing it was overpowered, turned and fled. The one-eyed dragon joined it, with Hun Kanny giving chase. However, due to the torture he had endured over Stackingsdale Bridge, he could not catch them as quickly as he had expected. Then, before he had gained much ground, he saw where the two dragons were headed, and he simply turned around. They were not making their way to Maine. They could hardly face the Red Dragon now. No, they were fleeing back to Bashaan.

When Hun Kanny returned to the island, the people cheered for their black beast of a guardian. But they were not cheering for him alone. They were also cheering for Samuel, the rock-throwing champion, who had saved the schwah prince by putting out the dragon's eye.

Samuel had no time to bask in glory. Hun Kanny was leaving in search of Jim. And Samuel knew that now was the time to take Calapanta back from the clungens. He had all islanders who were capable of battle load onto the boats and set out to the mainland.

Chapter Seventeen

HUN KANNY,
JIM, AND THE RED DRAGON

THE RED Dragon searched up and down the river. Then it began circling the area, inspecting Stackingsdale with its keen eyes. The more of the town it covered the more baffled it became by this mysterious riddle: "How could the schwah just disappear?"

Meanwhile, the clungens continued looking for Jim. Luntha took this opportunity to lure many of them to the same opening Jim had taken into the forest. Once entering the quagmire of branches, they were never seen again. The Impids made certain of that.

The Red Dragon remained oblivious to all of this as it anxiously searched for Hun Kanny. Then something happened that grabbed its attention. Clungens began pouring through the doorway from Calapanta. It could hear their shrieks of terror as they scrambled across the school's roof. They spoke of a black beast destroying all in its path, and it was coming to Maine. They had barely escaped its wrath, but it was certainly coming.

Once Luntha heard this, he slipped back into the woods to tell Kor. Neither of them could be sure what to make of this new beast. According to the clungens' reactions, it appeared to be more dreadful than the dragon itself. Kor decided to wait under cover of the forest to discover if the monster were friend or foe. For the sun was slow in setting; it was not time to attack Stackingsdale just yet.

The dragon, on the other hand, quickly surmised that this thing terrifying its clungens, this new beast, must be Hun Kanny. It was unable to solve the mystery, bewildered as to how Hun Kanny could have returned to Calapanta, but of its conclusion it had no doubt: the black terror *was* Hun Kanny. And the Red Dragon vowed that it would finish him this time around. Of course, it knew that Hun Kanny was far too intelligent to be caught at the doorway again, so it must lure him to its throne where it would pin him to the ground. Then it could have its feast.

****

MEANWHILE, JIM no longer sat staring into the dimming sky. He was kneeling on the roots and praying to God. There was no response. Growing desperate, he continued imploring Him to give him strength. The silent sky had been understandable, but *this* silence was unbearable. And he felt weak; he felt weak and empty... terribly empty. The longer he knelt, the more the roots dug into his kneecaps, and the weaker he felt. Frustrated, he pounded his fist into the dead leaves in front of him. It was then that he heard a splash. Something had struck the water while he was striking the earth. When he looked to see what it was, he saw a bird flying away carrying an object in its talons. The prey was dark, round, and solid, and Jim immediately remembered the baby turtle. He should feel sad, he thought; instead he shook his head in wonder and laughed. "Well, that's the end of the turtle," he said aloud.

Suddenly life didn't seem so bad. "So, I'm weak," he thought. "So what." The bird dropped the baby turtle, splitting its carapace on a large rock. Then it descended to collect its meal. "And turtles die," he mused.

As he observed this little episode in nature, he began to see that he was indeed a quitter. He had been a quitter all his life. He had quit baseball in sixth grade, football in eighth grade, and hockey last year. It was not the knee surgery – that was the excuse – it was the sitting on the bench that he was quitting. He could think of several teachers he had quit on. And he was quitting again.

He began to think of the actions that had led him here. He knew he should have stayed inside that basement. He knew that the Red Dragon would have been defeated if he had. But he hadn't. Instead he thought of how brave he had been to jump off the bridge when he had no other option and of the courage it took to walk through the cave... and, leaving the basement, he quit on Samuel.

He began to wonder why he hadn't been captured with his family in the first place, why the clungens had passed him by. He could clearly remember that they had seen him. They had stared at him with their bright red eyes and had taken aim.

And then they had shot him... "Wait – did they?" he questioned. "That never happened." And then he remembered jumping off a cliff. "No, it was a bridge," he thought to himself. But this time, he had jumped and soared over the sea. Surely, that had taken some courage. But he knew that hadn't happened either. He remembered flying in the night sky and then everything going black. Yes, he fell, and he clambered up in the darkness... But he couldn't place any of these memories. He had stolen a cloak. It wasn't his, but he *had* to have it, much as he *had* to help fight the dragons when he stole away from the basement. And he remembered hiding the cloak under his bed, and his mother waking him...

"The dream!" he exclaimed to himself. It was as if a dark veil had been removed from his eyes. All these visions suddenly made sense, and he recalled the dream he had had the night his family was captured. At first this shocked him. He couldn't understand why it was coming back so strongly, especially now. But as he allowed it to unravel before him, his mind began to see things it had never seen before. The dream had not been some strange coincidence of neurons randomly firing into his subconscious at the same time as his family was being taken away. It was too perfect. It had been a gift. From beginning to end, it had been a gift. Everything in it was meant for him to arrive at this point! From the planning and scheming to steal what wasn't his to the total dependence on the woman when he was helpless to save himself – it had all been too real. And he was ashamed that it had taken him this long to learn his lesson. But now he got it. Now he finally got it. It was not *his* bravery, it was not *his* courage that had enabled him to do anything that might be construed as heroic.

No, he was a coward. That much was evident. He was a weakling and a quitter. It was never him; it was *her*.

Why had he forgotten about her? When he first saw the Red Dragon, why hadn't he called on her as he had done in his dream? He didn't know the answer. But he was calling upon her now. Once again, *she* was the gift that was being given him.

"So, that's it," he said to himself in amazement. "That's all I needed to do!"

Then, laughing at his own stupidity, he rose to his feet. "Sometimes I can be a bit thick in the head," he admitted, speaking to the woman from his dream. After that, he left the dam and made his way back to Stackingsdale.

The time to meet the dragon had come.

****

BACK IN Stackingsdale, the wait was on. All the excitement and clamor had settled into an anxious anticipation. The sun dipped below the horizon. Then, without warning, a great fireball descended from the invisible doorway in the sky, lighting the rooftop of the school. Hun Kanny immediately burst forth, dark and terrifying, from within its flames. The clungens fled for their lives. But there was no escape. The schwah prince was riled into a Berserker rage, twisting and turning in every direction, spinning out of control. The fire sprayed in a spiral outwards, catching the clungens as they ran. But as the circle of fire extended itself further and further, his crazed frenzy began slowly to calm; there was no dragon. His furor was driven by a desire to find Jim, fully expecting to find him dead. This expectation had piqued his energy with an adrenaline rush of frenetic anger. He burst through ready to combat the Red Dragon. But the clungens were the only ones around – loathsome, ghoulish clungens. No Jim, no dragon could be seen. He surveyed the area, confused by their absence, looking for answers, and he noticed the tall building across the river – the tall building that used to be a church. It was occupied, which he found peculiar... seductively peculiar. The soft, red glow beckoned him to it.

Meanwhile, the Impids, energized by the appearance of Hun Kanny, were ready for battle. Kor had been just as perplexed as the dragon by the turn of events, but he knew that this black beast he saw killing and scattering the clungens could be none other than the mighty schwah prince. He led a charge into town, taking half of his Impids with him. The clungens who had survived Hun Kanny's attack caused them no difficulty. These creatures, so fearsome when supported by the dragon, were quite cowardly if left to their own devices. They ran before Kor's confident army in a mad panic, fleeing to the forest where they met with the Impids who had remained there. The way to the bridge was soon cleared of any obstacles, and Kor hurried to cross it, for he knew what was in the large building on the other side.

They could see Hun Kanny approach the building, and Kor screamed for his attention, cautioning the schwah not to go in, but he was far too distant to be heard. He then began shouting at the top of his lungs. "Stop!" he cried over and over, but to no avail; not one word reached Hun Kanny's ears.

A flame burst forth from the open doorway, followed by the deep, unmistakable voice of the dragon. "I've been waiting for you," it mocked. "Your boy and I have been waiting for you." Then it laughed its menacing laugh, attempting to rile Hun Kanny. "I have kept him alive, still willing to work the trade."

Then the massive doors shut.

Hun Kanny did not trust the dragon. If Jim were alive in that building he would have been able to sense it. And he could think of no reason the dragon would let Jim go free. There was only one possibility, he concluded. And this conclusion drove Hun Kanny livid with rage. Impetuously, he smashed the tremendous doors in. The Red Dragon had prepared for this. In fact it had depended upon it, and the snare had been set. When Hun Kanny flew through the doors, he was enveloped in a web of chains that had been attached to large metal plates bolted to the floor. Before he could react to the trap, he was caught, pinned to the ground.

The Red Dragon knew that the great links of the iron chain would be a short-lived restraint. Hun Kanny would soon break through. And presently, the chain was too awkwardly wrapped around him for the dragon to have a clear shot at his chest. It hadn't won yet, but it was the only one who knew this. Out on the bridge, Kor's hopes, the hopes of all the Impids, had been dashed by what they saw; but Kor continued to run, leading his army toward the building. He couldn't help feeling that he was leading them to certain death, but he found himself repeating what he had told Jim earlier: "We can't give up!"

And hope was indeed holding on, but only by the thread of Hun Kanny's awkward position. The dragon had wanted to tear the schwah's heart out as soon as he entered the building... to rip it out while he was still alive. This, it thought, would involve the greatest satisfaction as well as the least risk. In its haste to trap the schwah the dragon had been a bit reckless; it had failed to consider the manner in which he would become entangled in the chain. Since going straight for the heart was no longer an option, a more dangerous approach was now required. It would have to kill Hun Kanny first, and this it regretted. It did not, however, hesitate to attack, hoping for a quick death. The dragon went for his throat. It would choke the life out of the schwah.

The struggle was short. The iron chain had forced Hun Kanny into a somewhat supine position, though his back was not flat on the building's floor. His head was restricted by the chains as well. When he attempted to defend himself with fire of his own, he merely succeeded in torching the shattered doors, the ceiling, and the red windows to his left and right. He could not rebuff the dragon crouched in front of the altar. And soon the dragon had its claws wrapped around Hun Kanny's formidable neck. Then it proceeded to consume his head and neck in a fiery blanket. Obsessed with its blind revenge, the Red Dragon refused to let go though it was burning its own flesh. It held on as the flames continued rippling down the schwah's chest and onto his legs. As Hun Kanny weakened, the sensation of pain eventually overwhelmed the dragon's fear, and it was forced to release his neck so it could finish him within its flames. Then, as the fire raged on, the mighty schwah prince and protector of Calapanta could struggle no longer. His black and beaten body finally went limp.

The dragon grabbed Hun Kanny's neck once more. But before it could pounce on the schwah prince's body to finish him, it felt itself impeded by a bombardment of arrows, many of which managed to pierce its skin between the scales. It looked up and saw the Impids firing at it through the broken doors. To destroy them, it would be forced to release Hun Kanny.

This was no mere black dragon that would fearfully free its victim when attacked. No, it was the Red Dragon, and it would not loose its prey lightly. While holding Hun Kanny firmly in its grasp, it blew fire at this new enemy. It was a powerful blast, and the dragon hoped that the steady river of flames flowing forth through the doorway would be enough to frighten these pests away, giving it time to finish the schwah. The Impids *were* forced to seek cover, waiting for the fire to cease, but they did not run away. Once the fire stopped, they returned to assault the dragon with a second barrage of arrows. The dragon knew then what it must do. It gave one more blast. This blast was stronger than the first. It was also shorter. The bright fire went out instantly, and the Impids could see nothing in the ensuing darkness. The dragon took advantage of their temporary blindness and flew through the building's opening before their eyes could adjust. It continued to grip the schwah's neck, fighting against the chains anchored to the floor. Before the Impids could respond to this delay, it gave another short blast and pressed forward ripping the mighty bolts free. Then it rose into the night sky clasping its enchained prize.

For a few seconds, the dragon flew powerfully through the air. Then it began to look like a bird holding onto a fish too heavy to carry to its nest. Awkwardly gripping onto the schwah's neck, its claws began losing their hold of the dead weight beneath. The dragon had burned its hands so severely that they could no longer clutch as it desired. It was forced to descend back to earth, landing in the clearing just shy of the forest line. The arrows that showered upon the beast as it landed looked to be but an irritating nuisance, almost a waste of time; but looks can indeed be deceiving. As long as the Impids in the woods continued to pelt the dragon, it could not achieve its goal. Instead it blew fire into the forest in an attempt to protect itself while transferring the schwah to its hind legs. Hun Kanny was obviously dead, so the dragon, considering the slight risk, decided to hold him around his torso instead of by his neck. The even distribution of weight would make it easier to fly. But it was having a difficult time; the bombardment from the forest was slowing it down. And as it let go of Hun Kanny's neck, the thought of the schwah's unrestrained head frightened it, and it hurried to grip his body with its hind claws so that it could quickly fly away. In rushing, it became clumsy, and, consequently, took longer to escape with its prey.

It was at this moment, as the dragon was preparing its flight with Hun Kanny, that Jim came running from the forest. He didn't know what was happening and was horrified with the sight that greeted him. The moon was shining quite brightly by this time, and he could clearly see the Red Dragon clutching at Hun Kanny's black body, wrapped in chains, beneath it. But compelled by his mission and convicted by the force that urged him on, he continued running. He knew what it would take to slay the dragon, and time was running out. It was too late to rely on his own strength; the dragon, which had been delayed by the Impid attack, was now nearly ready. Jim yelled for a sword, but found it difficult to grab the Impids' attention. The few who did glance his way quickly turned back to continue shooting arrows at the dragon. They had seen him at the dam and were not ready to give this coward their weapon.

Jim continued running toward the dragon. He knew what the Impids must be thinking, and understood. Here was someone who had manifested nothing but cowardice, from meeting Kor near the river to meeting Kor at the dam, and now had the audacity to ask for their weapon. Of course they wouldn't give one to him. How could he blame them? There was no way they could possibly know the force that drove him on; that she would never let them down. Surely, they would trust *her,* if they only knew.

He reached the last line quickly. This was his final chance for a weapon. "Your sword!" he yelled to an Impid. The Impid, who appeared to be in charge, looked back at him. "Your sword!" Jim continued beseeching him, "Trust me! Please trust me!" Something in Jim's voice affected the Impid. There was a resolve he recognized as he watched Jim run full speed toward the fire-breathing dragon, a resolve he had felt just two days earlier when he had been sent on an especially dangerous covert reconnaissance mission. And he did trust Jim.

Vort handed his sword over, as Jim continued running toward the dragon.

Consumed with its purpose and distracted by the arrows with which it was being assailed, the dragon failed to notice the adolescent boy behind it sprinting toward its tail. Jim slid under the dragon's stomach and wriggled up to its chest. He could feel himself going faint with fear and closed his eyes tightly as he hid beneath its tremendous girth. Then, hoping beyond reason, trusting that he would not faint, he reached up and held onto the scales covering the dragon's chest.

The red beast flew away, leaving the Impids shooting at a target that was quickly out of range. It was only then that it noticed Jim clinging to it. He was holding on tightly, kicking his feet up to lodge them under its scales. There was nothing it could do about it; Jim was using the same tactic Hun Kanny had used so many years ago. The dragon's fat arms simply could not swat Jim away.

Jim's feet were finally secure under the scales, and he held on with one hand. The other slashed at the dragon's chest with Vort's sword. The scales seemed impenetrable. But he continued violently cutting away at the beast's armor. Meanwhile, the dragon, annoyed at its uninvited guest and fearful that Hun Kanny might revive at any moment, quickly spotted a tall hill on the other side of the river and flew for it. It was actually a miniature mountain. Trees surrounded its rocky summit. During the day one could view most of the city from this peak. But Jim was paying it no heed. He was focused entirely on cutting out the dragon's heart, and he was beginning to make some headway. Had he seen where the dragon was taking them, he wouldn't have recognized it anyway, having never viewed it from the sky.

The dragon finally landed. Immediately it threw Hun Kanny's dead body down the rocky edge. Jim looked over his shoulder. In the bright moonlight, he could see his guardian's limp corpse crash and then roll down the hill, as the chains unraveled. It came to rest, unfettered yet lifeless, against a rotting tree trunk lying in front of a boulder at the bottom. He now knew where he was, and once again, he remembered his dream.

A thick line of clouds slowly crept over the horizon as the dragon grasped at its chest. Its corpulence continued to prevent it from performing the simple task of grabbing the boy. Flustered by its own inability, it began blowing fire down its front, attempting to incinerate Jim. But it could not attain the needed angle and succeeded only in singing his hair. It was growing flustered, recognizing its danger. It knew it was giving Hun Kanny too much time to recover, yet if it did not stop this boy, he would soon be through its scales and at its heart. Then it hit upon a solution and was annoyed at its own idiocy for taking so long to recognize it: let something else tear this nuisance away. It dove down the hill toward a tree at the bottom, intending to crush the boy. When Jim saw what was happening, his heart stopped, but he did not let go. Then, just prior to impact, he leaped off the beast pushing himself to the side. He landed hard on his back but remained conscious. And as he looked to his side, he saw his guardian; Hun Kanny lay next to him.

The schwah prince turned his head and blindly reached for his boy – blind for he could not open his eyes. He was slow and weak, but alive. Seeing this, the Red Dragon knew it must finish Hun Kanny before wasting any more time with the boy. It knew how quickly the schwah could regain his strength. And the moon disappeared, consumed by the blanket of clouds, as the dragon fell upon the schwah prince to consume his heart. The time for victory had come. It clutched at his chest with its sharp claws. Though greatly weakened, they still managed to penetrate his skin and break through the ribcage. The Red Dragon could feel the heart beating on his fingertips. It was in ecstasy... a delirious ecstasy! And its own heart beat feverishly, pulsating through his body, through his fingertips. These two beats, separated by the thin layer of burnt reptilian skin, battled each other as the dragon itself reached deeper, reached to grip the heart in its palm, reached to tear it from within Hun Kanny's ribcage. With its prize literally in the palm of its hand, the Red Dragon lost sight of all else. Revenge was to be his. And it would be complete!

It was then, in this darkening night, as the dragon was on the verge of consummating its victory, that Jim managed to thrust Vort's sword through the scales at which he had slashed during the flight to Lookout Rock. The Red Dragon's claws gripped round Hun Kanny's heart. They tore it free, and the beast held it up in the face of the darkened sky. Jim, letting forth an incoherent, barbaric groan, forced his body against the sword, plunging it deep into the beast's heart. The dragon stood upright, blood red against the black sky. Then its body went into convulsions, one hand reaching, clutching helplessly, for the sword in its breast. But its eyes were affixed to the prize held in the other. Finally, the Red Dragon, the foul beast of Hummingbird Lake, fell backward onto its wings, crushing them beneath its tremendous weight. And when the dying was complete, it lay against the splintered rock, holding Hun

Kanny's heart in its lifeless hand, staring at it with lifeless eyes. Next to it lay the schwah prince's own dead body.

Tears streamed down Jim's cheeks as he frantically struggled to cut out the beast's punctured heart. He was fearful that the thing could yet come back to life. When he finally dislodged it from within its chest cavity, he heaved it into the darkness, where it landed amongst some fallen trees to rot with them at the base of Lookout Rock. Then he turned to his guardian and stared into the gaping hole in his chest. For some reason this hole was much greater than the one in the beast next to him. This hole was sadness and beauty; it was Hun Kanny's sacrifice, and Jim didn't know how to return the gift. Then he turned to the dragon. In its hand, so close to Hun Kanny it was almost touching his chest, it held Jim's gift. This suddenly seemed blasphemous, sacrilegious, and he attempted to dislodge the heart from within the beast's grip. It was more difficult than he had expected, for the Red Dragon's mighty claws had been clutching it with a yearning desperation.

When he finally pried the heart free, pulling back the claws using Vort's sword, he turned back to Hun Kanny unsure of what to do next. Then a curious inspiration came upon him, and he pressed the heart through the gaping hole in his guardian's chest. He hugged Hun Kanny close to *his* heart, squeezing him with all his might, hanging onto the hope that his own beating heart would resuscitate Hun Kanny's... that the mighty schwah prince would yet come back to life. He waited. Time ticked by. Seconds became minutes. Minutes turned into an hour, and the dark clouds in the sky let forth a torrent of rain.

Hun Kanny's body remained still and lifeless. Slowly, Jim realized it was over. He did not have the power to do what he was trying to do. Only One has.

He continued to lie there on the drenched earth hugging the schwah's body. Meanwhile, something was coming his way. He could hear it navigating through the darkness. He fully expected it to be a clungen but was unaffected. Clungens no longer mattered. They were as old as yesterday; the worst they could do was to kill him.

It was not until Kor walked up, making his way through the last dark trees, that he responded. "Will he come back?" he asked Kor, lifting his head from Hun Kanny's chest, "Do you know if he can come back?"

"I'm sorry," was the response. "No, I don't." Then Kor stood silently beside Jim.

Chapter Eighteen

CAVES AND FREEDOM

VORT LED his Impid warriors into Calapanta as soon as they heard the dragon was dead. They knew that without the red beast any surviving clungens in Maine would soon be taken care of, being no match for Kor's army. It was in Calapanta, they thought, that the serious fighting remained. Luntha, the only one who knew the country they were entering, went with them. When they arrived in the desert, however, there was no one to fight. They felt as if they had taken a wrong turn somewhere. Even Luntha felt lost. Vort leaned against the very boulder to which Luke had been brought two nights earlier, trying to decide where to go from here. After all, *this* was supposed to be the hot spot, the connection between the two realms. But it remained empty. There was nothing, nothing but the charred earth beneath their feet. It was not until an Impid went out into the chilly night to survey the area that they discovered any news. When he came back, he explained that the rocky terrain in the distance was littered with dead clungens, killed by Hun Kanny.

Dawn began to glow on the horizon, and for a few minutes the landscape grew hazier, darker even. Then, when the light shone across the harsh desert, they could see that the Impid had not been mistaken. Clungen corpses speckled the wasteland. It was only then that Luntha summoned up the courage to speak. "I know where the dragon's lair is," he said to Vort. "I could lead you to it."

"Why didn't you say something before?" asked Vort.

"Because I know what's in there," he answered, "And I'm not anxious to see it." He turned away, looking into the eastern horizon.

After a long pause, Luntha finally turned back to face Vort: "Caves," he said. "There are many caves... barred to prevent the slaves from escaping. They wouldn't let them go free." He shook his head sadly, "No... if they knew they were losing, they would never let them go..." He looked deep into Vort's eyes, "They would murder them."

"But the dragons didn't know they were losing," countered Vort. "They thought they were winning. In fact, they thought they were winning until the moment they lost."

"I'm not talking about dragons... and they're filled with hate. Those things, dead out on the desert plain, are filled with hate... what I almost became." And he spit in disgust. Then he turned away. "Are you ready to go?"

"Yes," answered Vort, nodding slowly.

Vort gave orders that the Impids were to follow Luntha to the dragons' lair, and Luntha started walking. As they began their journey, the first group of Calapantan islanders could be seen in the distance. They had not slowed down all night, across the channel, over the mountains, and through the desert. Rushing in the direction toward which they had seen Hun Kanny fly, they were prepared to fight any remaining clungens, but they had yet to meet any... until now.

Vort quickly explained their situation, as well as the situation in Maine. The cheers were instantaneous. Only Samuel, the friend of Hun Kanny, remained more somber. He waited for the islanders to calm down and then asked Vort, "And what is a clungen doing with you?"

Luntha held his silence in the face of the accusation, allowing Vort to do the speaking. "He was a human clungen... not quite unsalvageable, you know what I mean?" Vort didn't wish to go into the specifics of Luntha's conversion, thinking it unnecessary and inappropriate.

Samuel, however, found it quite necessary. None of the islanders knew of "human clungens," and a clungen conversion was simply impossible. Nothing of this sort had been heard of before, not even in legend. Had Vort known what an astounding anomaly this was, he would surely have given more information. But he didn't, and as Luntha was the only one who knew the way to the dragon's lair, Samuel, albeit suspicious, was forced to follow him.

As they made their way to the caves, Samuel approached Luntha with some of his questions. Luntha hid nothing. He knew they had a right to his story.

First, he told Samuel about Luke. Then he said something odd. He said that although he lamented the boy's death, in a way it was the greatest gift he could have been given. Without it he would not have been saved. Rather, the Red Dragon's defeat would have meant his end. His naked skeleton body would have been numbered among the rest rotting on this charred earth. He went on to say that even though he had escaped the slavery of being a clungen, he was not yet at peace. His cowardice, he added sorrowfully, had harmed many who were close to him.

Luntha had abandoned his younger sister when his father left the family. In fact, Luntha had tried to convince her that she should join the dragons with him, that, without their father, it was the only choice they had. Young as she was, she had resisted. She could see hope where there was none, believing in the legends she had heard, the legends that he and his father rejected. And so he left her – he had known what would happen to her, as she pleaded with him through her imploring blue eyes, but he left her. He actually rationalized away leaving the one he loved to the cruel, inhuman whims of the dragon. He had felt too weak to battle the inevitable; there was nothing he could do to protect her anyway. In fact he had joined the very ones who would be torturing her. And when the Red Dragon asked where she was hiding, he told it – again, under the pretense that it was inevitable. She would be found anyway, so why should he suffer for it?

That was when the Red Dragon gave him the name "Luntha" and put him in his position of power. For what more could he do to manifest his complete subjection to the dragon? Because of this it had allowed him to remain human much longer than most; he was more useful that way. The final transformation, the living death, would remove his ability to tempt humans to their side.

And now everything he had done to help the dragons since then was a mountain weighing on him; if he were ever to have peace, he told Samuel, he must find his sister. But he was very much afraid she was already dead.

Luntha did not know with certainty that she was in the caves. The Red Dragon had never told him what it had done with her, and it had refused to allow him to see the prisoners. The caves were the "completed" clungens' domain. But he knew the dragons kept the prisoners alive, marveling at their strength. The thinking was that such strength, when turned to evil, could be exceedingly useful. The clungens, on the other hand, treated the prisoners with a malicious spite. They saw the strength that they, the clungens, lacked, and this filled them with an unquenchable envy. Even Luntha had hated the prisoners. If it weren't for the dragons, the clungens would have killed these captives on sight.

When Luntha was finished talking, Samuel asked for his real name, his birth name. "You can't know what it's like," was the response, "'Luntha' is the name I deserve."

****

THE SUN rose warmly into the sky behind them as they approached the caves. Entering immediately, they began the difficult search. They were forced to proceed slowly, not knowing the layout of this cavernous prison, depending on torchlight to negotiate its labyrinthine halls. As they called out, shouting to anyone who might hear, heralding their freedom, they began to lose hope. Each yell was met with its return echo and then with silence.

"She was so strong," Luntha told himself, as he observed this silent response to deliverance. "The Red Dragon wouldn't have wanted to lose her strength." He was attempting to ignore the meaning behind those hollow echoes, the reverberations falling on dead ears. "She was so strong... so very strong," he repeated.

Then came the disheartening news. Cell after cell of murdered bodies was found. There were more than Luntha had imagined, many more than the Red Dragon had ever admitted. And these heroes had not been burned to death by dragons. It was just as Luntha had foretold. Realizing the end was near, the clungens had used their spears and swords and knives to slaughter as many humans as possible in a bloodthirsty, mindless rampage that was to be their last destructive act in Calapanta. And it forced Luntha to the ground. Not wanting to see his dead sister's butchered body lying on the floor of a rank prison cell, he covered his face with his hands, and, once again, he wept. His sister, he moaned, didn't deserve this violent, this cruel, death. It was purely diabolical, just as Luke's had been... and he was responsible for both of them. The evil he had done was crushing him under its unbearable weight, and he began to despair of any dreams of peace.

SUDDENLY, SHOUTS of joy were heard from the deepest pits of the cave – happy cheers, out of place within such dismal halls. They continued to ring, unabashed, through the somber darkness, but Luntha remained unmoved. He was too absorbed in his own forlorn thoughts, deaf to this change of fortune. It was only when his shoulders were violently shaken by Samuel that he snapped out of it. The words

"Alive! There are still some alive!" sounded foreign, a jumbled sentence from a strange dream. He looked up, struggling to make sense of what was being said and was met with the joyous glee of the freed prisoners, hastening toward the sunlight of the cave's mouth.

Then over Samuel's shoulder, he saw a family approaching. The father was walking up from the dark hall, his right arm wrapped around his wife, but the two looked unsettled, less cheerful than would be expected. To the left of the worried couple walked a teenaged boy. He was visibly concerned about something as well. He had just asked his father a question, and the man was answering: "I don't know, Pauly... I just don't know yet..."

Before Luntha heard what they were talking about he saw a young girl holding hands with the mother. He had seen her in his initial glance but had thought that she was their daughter. This time, however, their eyes met through the flickering torchlight, and he recognized his little sister. At first he didn't trust his eyes, thinking she was a vision. But when she recognized him as well, seeing through her brother's transformation, through the clungen he had almost become, she let go of the woman's hand, and, screeching with joy, threw herself into his arms. There was no spite in her innocent blue eyes as she wrapped her arms around his neck telling him how much she had missed him.

"Damian," she cried over and over until he could reject his name no longer, "Damian, I thought I would never see you again!"

And Damian hugged her tightly, afraid that if he let go, she would vanish like a dream into the darkness of the cave. And he wasn't going to let that happen again.

Chapter Nineteen

A FAMILY REUNION

KOR HAD brought several of his Impids with him to the base of Lookout Rock. And when Jim asked if they would help him drag Hun Kanny's body to the river, they agreed. It was a long journey through the woods and into town, especially for Jim. Waves of emotion swept over him as his thoughts drifted from the schwah prince's death to victory over the Red Dragon to his lost family – it was this last thought that was the most difficult to handle. But he refused to give in, feeling that he owed it to Hun Kanny to maintain his composure. He kept reminding himself to "put one foot in front of the other" until his mind gradually went numb. The monotonous repetition carried him to the bridge free of any emotional breakdowns.

The body was laid on the road in the middle of Memorial Bridge, and Kor asked Jim if there were anything he wished to say before they dropped Hun Kanny's body into the river. Jim silently shook his head. He knew that if he tried to speak he would lose control. And, besides, he could think of no words that would be worthy of the mighty schwah prince who had been his guardian. So, silently and reverently, the body was raised over the rails and let go.

Jim looked without emotion, almost apathetic, as he stared blankly into the water, watching his childhood fantasy disappear beneath the tremendous splash it created. "Jim," Kor said, attempting to get his attention. Jim waited for the ripples to reach the river's banks where they slowly dissipated before he looked up at Kor. "Jim, you were never meant to jump into the river that morning."

"I know," Jim answered, turning to look out over the flowing water. "I just don't understand."

"Maybe we never will..." Kor was staring down the river as well. "I need to get going, Jim... My parents are waiting for me." He continued to watch the water flowing on. "I need to get back for my brother's funeral." Kor's voice was shaking, but he kept his poise, his eyes fixed on the water.

Then, spontaneously, as if shaken himself by Kor's words, Jim reached out and hugged Kor, and before he realized that he had done it, he was squeezing him tightly, whispering, "Thank you, Kor, thank you."

"I'm not the one who deserves it," he answered, hugging Jim back. He was thinking of his brother's sacrifice and remembering the blue eyes he had seen on the mountainside. The two were united, the sacrifice and those eyes, mysteriously intertwined in his mind now, never to be separated. He thought of his parents as well; he thought of them sitting in the church with Luke. "I pray you find your family," he whispered to Jim. Then they let each other go.

Kor left with his Impids. They made their way back to the dam from which they had come. Jim remained on the bridge for a time, not imagining how quickly Kor's prayer was to be answered.

IT WAS the earthquake that stirred Jim from his thoughts. He was surprised at first, but then he remembered what Samuel had told him, and he knew what was happening. The Red Dragon was being swallowed into the bowels of the earth. After only a few seconds, the shaking ceased, and he let go of the railing he had grabbed when the earthquake began. The Red Dragon was gone. All was calm once more.

The time had come to find his family.

Jim knew that his best chance to find them was in Calapanta. Forcing himself to leave the bridge, he walked toward the school. For the first time he was able to soak in the destruction that had decimated the town. He looked around but did not recognize Stackingsdale. The school, the buildings along either side of the bridge, the cars along the street, all were in ruins, destroyed by the fire. The skeleton bodies of dead clungens decorated the burnt landscape like a scene from a cheesy horror movie. Everything was different... changed. The school year just beginning had been abruptly ended. And he wondered what his life would become, unsure of what to expect on the other side of the doorway. Then he went through. Last night, coming the other way, he had been far too frightened and the dragon had been flying far too quickly for Jim to remember anything he had seen. Even if he did remember, he still would have been unprepared. For his family was approaching on the other side.

They were unprepared as well – joyfully stunned at the sight of Jim. They had been hurrying to the doorway, anxious to look for him in Maine, unsure of what to expect. Damian had told them of Jim's request for Vort's sword during the battle against the dragon. He told of Jim's courageous charge toward the dragon itself. But he was ignorant of the boy's fate. The Red Dragon was dead, along with Hun Kanny. Of that much he was certain. But he had heard nothing else of the struggle on Lookout Rock. Hearing this, the father had reminded the family that there was always hope, not to lose hope.

Such was their state as they approached the boulder. At the sight of Jim, the torment of uncertainty melted away in a reunion of tearful hugs, laughter, and joy. The nightmare had ended.

When coherence was finally possible, Jim was introduced to the young girl who was with them. He was told that her name was Natasha and that they had met her in the darkness of their prison. Both of her parents had been killed in the war. "And this is her brother," Jim's mother said referring to Damian. "But I believe you've already met."

"Yes, we have," replied Jim with an awkward smile. "But I don't think he was very impressed." Damian appeared to ignore the comment as he heartily shook Jim's hand.

ARRANGEMENTS WERE quickly made. The details would be ironed out over time. Jim's parents were to take Natasha in as their daughter. When Damian was asked for his approval, he said that he was her brother, not her father. Yes, she needed parents.

Not long after the Red Dragon's death, the doorway above the school building began to weaken. As it became more and more difficult to traverse, Damian was forced to make a decision. Desiring to remain near his sister, he took up his residence in Maine. Soon after, the doorway disintegrated entirely.

****

THE NEXT few months were difficult... terribly difficult. Few had survived in Stackingsdale, Maine. In fact, the clungens had nearly emptied Cobbossee County. But the survivors had returned to paste their lives back together.

When the TV cameras flew in – many more than last time; for this wasn't merely the disappearance of a single family; an entire town had been mysteriously destroyed – the story of the dragons was promptly discarded. Yes, something dreadful had obviously occurred. Something so dreadful, in fact, that for most of the town's population the burnt skeletons of the anonymous dead were all that remained. (That these skeletons were actually clungen corpses was an unbelievable idea finding print only in the national tabloids, which never quite grasped the idea of a "clungen" in the first place.)

It was the specialists who slowly pieced together a more likely scenario – slowly, for the stories coming out of Stackingsdale were not to be trusted. Whatever had occurred, it had disturbed the townspeople to the point of mad hallucinations.

This "more likely scenario" consisted of a plague-like disease sweeping through Cobbossee County, Maine, killing its victims swiftly. In the panic that ensued, the town hastened to burn the bodies of the dead to prevent the living from contracting the disease. The flames quickly grew out of control setting much of the town on fire.

There were many who refused to believe such fantastic explanations. The tabloids adhered to their own ideas of dragons and doorways to mysterious realms. The majority of the media, however, refrained from adhering to either story. They concluded that it would take years of combing through the debris before arriving at a reasonable cause. As for the townspeople, they were understandably grieved but, upon further study, were found to be mentally stable. Yes, they refused to yield on the subject of their hallucinations, but other than that, considering the horrific nature of the event they had survived, they were adjusting better than could be expected.

It was the "disease" that caused more concern. Science teams came from around the world to study the remains of the infected bodies. After inspecting the skeletons they concluded that the disease was indeed real. And nothing comparable had been seen before. It appeared to consume the entire body, leaving no part untouched. This news bred a fear that swept across the nation. But as time passed no cases were reported, and dread of this "plague" gradually dissipated.

Its origin remained unknown.

THE LARGE building was renovated, and the tabernacle was ceremoniously placed behind the altar once again, completing its conversion back to a Catholic church.

The opening mass was a requiem. Damian sat with Jim's family for the emotional occasion. And when it ended they made their way home.

The six of them went into the living room. Pauly played cards on the coffee table with Natasha, while their parents and Damian sat on the couch together, talking. Jim, however, was mulling over the war. There was something he had never told his family, and it troubled him.

He turned to his parents interrupting them, "I'm no hero. You know that, right?"

His mother was perplexed, as was Damian. Pauly and Natasha looked awkwardly up at him, forgetting their cards. But his father remained undisturbed.

"When my time to be a hero came, I was asked to sit in a basement. That's all. That's all it would have taken to be a hero." Everyone remained silent. Jim obviously held the floor, so he continued. "If I could've sat there, it would have been the bravest thing I'd ever done. But now there are still two dragons out there..."

"Hold on," it was his father's turn to interrupt, "It happened just as it was meant to. I want you to understand that. You made a mistake. So, you're human. That's an important lesson." He smiled. "Welcome to humanity!" He ruffled Jim's hair. "Sure, there are two dragons out there somewhere, but their time will come." Jim wasn't exactly sure why this made him feel much better. But it did. The relief his dad provided with a few simple words was just part of being a father, he guessed.

"Thanks Dad," he said. Then he told Natasha not to beat Pauly too badly, excused himself, and went to his bedroom.

Chapter Twenty

HUMMINGBIRDS

A PLAIN-CAPPED Starthroat could be seen amongst the flowers of Hummingbird Lake. Peter was the first to spot the little bronze-green bird drinking in the nectar, and he ran to tell his father. Samuel rushed to the lakeside. By the time they arrived, six or seven smaller hummingbirds could be seen hovering in the flowers that grew next to the calm lake. Samuel could barely restrain his joy as he ran back to the village telling the islanders to come immediately. None of them was sure what this meant, but they came as quickly as they could.

In the distance, they could see the hummingbirds flitting around the waterfall. By now there were too many to count. Then, as if called by a silent voice, they flew to the center of the lake and hovered as one body, their low hum resounding along the shore. The villagers couldn't have known that they were waiting patiently to welcome their guardian home. And as he burst through the surface of the lake, the mass of hummingbirds covered him.

Samuel stood with his son Peter, watching with the other islanders. They were able to catch just a glimpse of Hun

Kanny's charred, black body as it bobbed above the water before the hummingbirds obstructed their view. They were reviving him, rejuvenating him... coloring him brilliantly. And when they finished caring for their majestic schwah prince, Hun Kanny laughed. He laughed at the amusing expressions on the stupefied faces of the villagers. He laughed joyfully, and his magnificent, beautiful body shook in laughter – a laughter that boomed across the lake, rippling the water on the distant shore with its sound waves.

And Jim had to put his pen down. He could no longer write, for he was laughing too. In fact, he was laughing so hard that his belly hurt as refreshing tears streamed down his face.

Made in the USA
Middletown, DE
23 August 2017